To ?

you are

I hope you enjoy
this one!

B x

LILIAN

CW01481313

Also by the same author

Just Julia -
  short stories.

Overheard in a Coffee Shop -
  thriller.

Wooden Dolls and Drunken Hedgehogs -
  an illustrated country diary

Published in 2017 by FeedARead.com publishing - Arts Council funded

Copyright Bernard Harvey

First Edition

.

To Dad, who started the rumour...

My grateful thanks to Mike for his help with the historical notes, Ann for being, as ever, a patient proof reader, Peter's editorial advice and finally, Kevin's fantastic cover!

Historical note

The summer of 1914 had hardly got under way when, at the end of June, the assassination of the Austrian Crown Prince Franz Ferdinand and his wife rocked Europe. The catastrophe which followed was mainly due to the alliances between certain countries that forced them into war.

The Austro-Hungarian government gave an ultimatum in strictest terms to Serbia, accusing them of collaborating with the Black Hand secret society who had provided the assassin.

Serbia, bolstered by an alliance with Russia, rejected the ultimatum, thus giving Austria-Hungary the excuse to declare war on 28th July. This was in the knowledge that they (Austria-Hungary) had an alliance with Germany, who would support them.

Russia mobilised, which was viewed by Germany as an act of aggression and they too promptly declared war.

France, bound by a treaty with Russia, caused Germany to act swiftly, incorporating the

Schlieffen plan to invade Belgium as a direct route to Paris.

Following an appeal for help from Belgium on August 4th 1914, Britain entered the war against Germany.

Prologue

'Helene, come away from the rail.'

The small blonde headed girl reluctantly obeyed her mother's command and made her way across the deck of the cross channel ferry to join her parents and her elder sister, where they perched on wooden seats.

The *Stad Antwerten*, with its steam turbines proudly driving her sturdily out to the harbour mouth, was a modern ship of its time. It could carry nearly nine hundred passengers as it sailed for Ostend. The two funnels belched smoke as the screws bit into the dark green waters of the English Channel.

'But Mummy, when will we see England again?'

'Soon, dear. We shall be back for Christmas.'

'Liebling, it all depends on my work.' Helene's father spoke softly but in a guttural voice to her mother.

'I know, but I am so worried about the children. Will they settle in Germany?'

Any chance of reply was drowned by the ferry's siren signalling their departure from the shelter of Dover's

harbour. The boat began to roll in the seasonal spring

weather.

'Do you think they will be happy?' persisted Ethel, the children's mother.

'Of course they will. Margaret already knows a little German and Helene will have to learn. Now let's get out of this wind. I know it's April next week, but it will be very chilly when we get out into the Channel and it's starting to rain again.'

Gathering up all their hand luggage, the family made their way to the stairs that took them down to the main saloon. Helene followed reluctantly after taking a last look at the white cliffs of Dover.

The band marching down the street in Berlin, blasted out martial music. Walter Pape threw down the paper he had been reading and strode across the room to the window pulling it firmly shut. His wife, Ethel, stared at the headlines on the paper her husband had thrown down.

'If it's war, what are we to do?'

Walter stood in front of his wife and spread his hands in despair. 'You and the girls must leave.'

'I can't leave without you,' she whispered.

'I've got my orders. In two weeks I'll be at the

Front and who knows when I'll get back.'

'We can wait here, in our home,' his wife replied.

'It won't be safe. If ever we are invaded, I hate to think what would happen to you and the girls.' Walter paused in thought. 'I doubt if you will be able to travel back to England. But… there is my Aunt Lotte, in Solothurn, Switzerland. You must take the children and stay with her.'

'What if they stop us leaving?'

'Why should they? As Frau Pape you are quite entitled to travel to Switzerland, a neutral country. Especially as you are going to stay with your children's aunt, who is German.'

'But none of us speak German.'

'Aunt Lotte speaks excellent English and French. She will make a very good tutor for the children.'

Helene lay on her back in the long grass watching how the summer breeze played with the Swiss flag flying over a nearby chalet. 'Do you realise, we have been here over three years? It is so beautiful. I could live here for ever and ever.' She rolled over on to her stomach and looked at her sister. Margaret, who was six years older than Helene and far more serious, was absorbed in her watercolour painting. 'Do you think Mother will come to see us soon?'

Margaret paused and regarded her work critically. Then turning to her sister she shook her head. 'I don't know. The war has been going badly for Germany. They say the frontier has been closed to stop the flood of refugees and any escaped prisoners.'

'How exciting. Perhaps we can rescue one.'

'Helene! You know how Aunt Lotte doesn't like us to discuss the war. It upsets her. She thinks we should all be in a form of union in Europe.' She paused to add a little more paint to the canvas. 'Did you know Napoleon was a firm believer in a European union for trade and Charlemagne wanted a union in Europe of all Christians, even if it was to fight the Turks?'

'I hate war!' Helene exclaimed vehemently, before sitting up and clasping her knees. For a few moments she chewed a long piece of grass as she studied her sister's work. 'That's very good,' she announced, changing the subject.

'Thank you. Aunt Lotte says that if we're still here next year when I'm seventeen, she will try and enrol me in the Art School.'

'Golly, maybe you will become famous, or marry a

famous artist. Or both!' Helene rolled back on the grass doubled up in laughter.

'Hardly likely.' Margaret peered over her glasses at her younger sister. 'Actually, you are quite pretty!' She turned back to her painting before adding 'For a child'.

Helene jumped up. 'You beast. I'm not a child. I'm nearly eleven. Anyway, I'm going to become a famous ballerina. My teacher says I have a natural talent.' She twirled on the grass before falling over in a giggling heap.

'Mm … we shall see. Now please don't keep interrupting, I want to finish this before the light goes.'

The year slid by and winter was setting in when, on a cold November day, the two girls made their way down to the small Alpine village. Well wrapped up, they battled against the fine snow that blew in from the east. Finally arriving at the shop, they entered the building to be met with a blast of warm air.

Helene greeted the lady behind the counter before making her way over to the cast iron stove. Taking off her gloves she warmed her hands over the fire. 'Ooh that's better.'

'Helene, bring me the basket. You've got the list that Aunt Lotte gave us.' Margaret stood impatiently at the counter, waiting for her sister. She turned to the lady behind the counter and apologised.

The shopkeeper smiled back. 'Not to worry. We are very quiet today.'

Margaret picked up a newspaper and struggled with the headlines. 'The Kaiser has fled Germany,' she read out loud. 'What does that mean? '

The lady shook her head. 'Germany is in turmoil. There has been a revolt in Kiev. It could mean an end to the war!'

Helene joined her sister at the counter and stared at the lady. 'The war is over?' she asked excitedly.

'No.' Margaret turned to Helene. 'It means that it may finish before the New Year.'

'Do you realise it will be 1919 next year. We have been here for over four years!'

Margaret hugged her sister. 'Maybe we shall see mother and father soon.'

'Do you think father is still alive?'

Margaret gave her sister a small shake. 'You mustn't think like that. Now where's the list, let's hurry up and get back to Aunt Lotte and tell her the news.'

Their aunt who was waiting at the door, had news of her own. In her hand was an envelope that she waved at the sisters. 'Girls, girls! I've had a letter from your mother. She's had news of your father.'

They quickly took off their coats and scarves before following their aunt through to the main sitting room where a cheerful log fire crackled in the grate.

'He's being sent home.' Aunt Lotte smiled reassuringly. 'Apparently he has had pneumonia and is getting better but needs to recuperate. Your mother expects him any day now. We shall make up a food parcel and send it to her.'

'Does that mean we shall be going home soon?' asked Helene excitedly.

Her aunt looked down at the letter she was holding in one hand. 'I think you will have to wait quite a bit longer. The conditions are very bad in Magdeburg. There is a huge shortage of food and the facilities are very bad according to your mother. She says she will come to visit us as soon as possible. She is also very pleased that Margaret is doing so well at the art college and insists that you continue your ballet lessons, Helene.'

Chapter 1

'Helene!' The name was barked out sternly. 'You must listen to what I say.' The speaker was a tall forbidding looking lady, dressed in long robes with her hair piled up on top of her head. For some time she watched the girls warming up by dancing to a variety of music. As she did so, she beat time gently on the grand piano. After five minutes she clapped her hands and the ballet troupe came to a standstill. After some words of encouragement the pianist started another exercise and the dancers responded under the strict gaze of their teacher.

This was the ballet and theatre school at Staatsoper, home of the Berlin State Opera which had recently reopened. Helene had just celebrated her eighteenth birthday and had at last joined her mother in Berlin, having progressed from the small ballet school in Switzerland to this brand new venture.

A girl entered the room, walked across to the ballet teacher and gave her an envelope. Waiting until the girl had left and still watching the dancers, she opened the envelope before reading the contents of the note inside. When the pianist finished the piece of music, the teacher clapped her hands again and the dancers, thankful for the break, came to a halt.

'Helene, put on something warm and then go to Herr Director's office. He wants to talk to you.'

Helene's heart sank; she knew her review was due and worst of all she guessed she had grown too tall to be a professional ballet dancer. There is no way to hide your height when you are dancing. Slowly she gathered up her clothes and made her way to the third floor and knocked on the Director's door.

'Come!'

Tentatively she opened the door.

'Ah Helene, come in, come in.'

Helene entered the room and took the seat she was offered. Rudolf Bayer was a kindly man and was quite aware how strict a regime the girls were under.

'Helene, I have been reading your report and I am sure that as much as you have learnt you will know that your height is now a problem.'

Helene must have looked crestfallen, because Herr Director held up his hands. 'But all is not lost. You will be well aware the school sends out a touring party every summer. We feel that you would be ideal in a part that requires modern dance and light operetta. Your tutor tells me you have a pleasant voice. So how do you feel about that?' He beamed at her.

Her face lit up. 'Oh … thank you, sir!' She blushed.' That is to say, I am very sorry about the ballet. I didn't mean to …'

'Helene, it is certainly not your fault that you have grown. That is a fact of mother nature. Now then, here are your course notes and you have an appointment to meet the tour director tomorrow morning at nine o'clock. Don't be late!'

'But Helene, you can't just change your name!'

'Lots of people do, especially actresses.' Helene banged the lid of her case shut and smiled at her mother. 'Anyway you haven't asked me what I intend to change it to. It might please you!'

'Oh?'

'From now on my stage name will be Lilian Harvey.'

Ethel stared at her daughter. 'Mother's maiden name. What ever made you think of that?'

'I don't know. I just like the name.' She laughed and hugged her mother. 'There, it sounds right and I know you chose Lilian as my second name.'

Her mother returned her hug and held her daughter at arm's length. 'Well, Miss Lilian Harvey, what time does your train leave?'

'At two o'clock. We have to meet Herr Heinrich at the station at one.'

'What is Herr Heinrich like?'

'Creepy! Not like dear old Rudolf. He was such a darling.'

'Do take care, Helene. I'm sorry I can't go with you.'

'Mother, I have a chaperone and there are ten other girls in the troupe.'

'It's not the girls I worry about!' Her mother picked up one of the cases and led the way out of the room.

The station was packed and with the troupe and their personal luggage were all their props and the supporting members. The girls chattered excitedly and the noise was bedlam until Herr Heinrich found his voice and shouted for silence. Eventually they boarded their reserved coach and twenty minutes later the steam train drew slowly out of the station.

Some hours later they arrived at their hotel in Vienna. That evening they were highly enthusiastic at the prospect of their first proper roles, even though they had two weeks of rehearsals to contemplate. Lilian found she was sharing a room with her friend Heidi, who had also switched from ballet to modern dance. Excitedly they talked late into the night.

The next morning a coach took them from their hotel to the venue. The girls regarded the slightly down-at-heel Ronacher Theatre with dismay.

'It's so seedy looking', whispered Lilian to Heidi.

'I know. It looks more like a brothel than a theatre', Heidi giggled, as they streamed off the coach. But the posters outside the theatre announcing their show cheered them up and they threw themselves into their work. They rehearsed until Lilian had to admit the show, *Wein. gib'acht (Vienna give eight),* had great promise.

The one drawback was Herr Director, Otto Heinrich.

Lilian's observation was proved more than accurate, having already described him as 'creepy', when, three days into their rehearsal, Lilian came across Heidi crouched in a corner, weeping quietly.

21

'Whatever's wrong, Heidi?' She dropped down beside her friend and put an arm around her shoulders. 'Come on, you can tell me.'

'Herr Heinrich. He said he could help me,' she sobbed.

'How?'

'Well you know I have always wanted to be in films and so I went to see Herr Heinrich and asked if it was possible. He said it was, especially as he knew a well known film director.'

'That's good. You'd be terrific.'

Heidi sniffed and shook her head. 'He said if I was nice to him and then he put his hand up my skirt ...', she sobbed again.

Lilian put her hand over her mouth. 'Oh my God! The dirty old man! I mean you hear of these things, but luckily we've Frau Hauptman who keeps this sort at arms' length. Have you told her?'

Heidi shook her head.

'Right. Well in future make sure you are never alone with Herr Heinrich and if he wants to talk to you, take Frau Hauptman or me with you. Now come, we have another hour before our next rehearsal, let's go and have a hot chocolate.'

The rehearsals went well and although the opening night wasn't exactly the glamorous night of things to come, the theatre was full and the show was well received. Lilian's looks, her voice and her skill as a dancer stood her in good stead. It was even more fortunate that just after her nineteenth birthday there happened to be a talent spotter in the audience who set the wheels in motion. So it wasn't a coincidence one morning when a well known German film director called in to see Otto Heinrich.

'Herr. Eichberg, what brings you to Vienna and our theatre today?' Otto Heinrich ushered the film director to a seat in the deserted stalls.

'I am just starting on a new film and I need to fill one or two parts. A friend told me you have some talented girls, although God knows why you hide them in this flea pit.' Richard Eichberg waved his hands around expansively.

Otto shrugged his shoulders. 'Beggars can't be choosers. But of course, any contribution to our funds would be very acceptable.'

'Mm, we shall see. Would it be possible to see a line-up of your troupe?'

'Er yes ... In about half an hour they will be here for a warm up before the matinee. Why don't we get some coffee and schnapps whilst we are waiting?'

'I must say it does seem you have quite a bit of talent here.' Richard gazed up at the troupe who were warming up on the stage with one of their dance numbers. 'What about that girl? The blonde in the blue dress, Herr Heinrich.'

'Please call me Otto. Now you mean Helene Pape, or rather she calls herself Lilian Harvey. Good actress and an excellent dancer.'

'How old is she?'

'Nineteen.'

Richard nodded. 'Pretty girl, a bit on the fluffy side, but would be ideal for the part I have in mind. Can she sing?'

'Of course. A sweet voice.'

'Better still.'

Otto simpered. 'Good. Would you like to meet her now?' He stood up and waved to the choreographer who was directing them on stage. 'Jens, send Lilian Harvey down here.'

Lilian left the rehearsal to join them in the stalls.

Otto put his arm around her. 'Lilian, this is Herr Eichberg. Now turn round and show off your lovely form.'

Lilian blushed and turned round with some embarrassment.

But the director stopped her. 'Lilian, a friend of mine was very impressed with your performance the other evening. Do you like stage work?'

'Yes, very much.'

'Have you done any screen work?'

Lilian shook her head.

Richard Eichberg smiled. 'Never mind. Well if you are interested, take my card and come to our local office tomorrow morning and we will give you a screen test.'

Lilian looked enquiringly at Otto who nodded his head approvingly.

'Thank you, Herr. Eichberg. What time?'

'Shall we say nine sharp?'

Lilian nodded her head and Richard smiled back; standing up he gathered his coat and draped it over his shoulders. 'Until tomorrow.' He bowed over Lilian's hand and dramatically swept out of the theatre.

Lilian clapped her hands in excitement and the troupe came down off the stage to see what all the fuss was about. Heidi hugged her whilst whispering, 'Be careful, Lilian. I suggest you take along Jens as a chaperone, he'll take good care of you.'

Chapter 2

In 1919, Adolf Hitler joined the German Workers' Party, which changed its name the following year to the National Socialist German Workers' Party, commonly known as the Nazi Party.

Ironically, because he was still in the army as an intelligence agent, this membership had to be approved by an army officer. Well known as a skilled orator and joining the party in its infancy, Hitler advanced quickly to join the committee.

By early 1923, Hitler had formed two organisations, one which would ultimately become the Hitler Youth, and the other the dreaded Schutzstaffel, or SS as it became known.

In November 1923, Adolf Hitler led the Beer Hall Putsch, an attempted coup d'etat. He was subsequently arrested for high treason, convicted and imprisoned. His time in prison was spent writing the first volume of Mein Kampf; the setting out of his political beliefs which were, over the next ten years, to form the basis of his supporters' growth. Released from prison within the year, Hitler now strove for power.

***

Early next morning, Lilian and Jens made their way by tram across the city of Vienna to the District of Lanstrasse where Richard Eichberg had an office.

'Thanks for coming with me, Jens.' Lilian smiled at her companion.

'It's no problem. Anyway I'm glad to be away from Otto. He spends his time finding fault with me, I suspect it's because I'm Jewish.'

Lilian thought of her friend Heidi and her predicament. 'I think he is an odious man. Besides, you're an excellent choreographer and who cares if you are Jewish?'

'Herr Hitler for one. He poisons the minds of the

German people.'

'Oh him! But he is supposed to have the whole of Germany at heart.'

Jens Keith shook his head. 'That's what he would like you to think. But his rants on anti-Semitism are well known and I sometimes fear for our future.

'Oh, Jens. Never forget you have a friend here. Perhaps I can get you a job with me. After all, you are my choreographer and if it wasn't for your work I might not have been spotted in the first place.'

Jens laughed. 'There's nothing like confidence! Ah here we are. As the Americans might say "Go get 'em, doll!", this is your big chance.'

They descended from the tram and made their way to the offices of Richard Eichberg.

The meeting was a great success and after a trial in the film *The Curse,* in which Lilian played the part of a young Jewish woman whose wild behaviour drives her screen mother to suicide, she was given a part in Richard Eichberg's film *The Motorist Bride.* Strangely, she played the stunt double for the female star, Lee Parry, in mountaineering scenes taken in Switzerland.

But it was the beginning and she quickly rose in

Richard Eichberg's stable to be given the lead in Eichberg's silent melodrama, *Passion,* in 1925. Success followed with a comedy film, *Love and Trumpets,* as Eichberg's motion picture machine produced one silent film after another. In 1926 she starred opposite Willie Fritsch for the first time, in the comedy, *The Chaste Susan*. A few years earlier, an English stage version known as *The Girl in a Taxi* caused quite a stir.

This on-screen romance with Willie Fritsch was to be repeated in many more films, particularly as talking pictures were attracting audiences in France and England, as well as Germany. One day, before the first takes of *Hocus Pocus,* Lilian was called in to the Director's office.

Richard waved her to a chair. 'Lilian, we want to do a English version of *Hocus Pocus*. Not just with dubbing but using an English cast and including you.'

'What about Willie?'

'Ah. We have found you a new leading man. He's new to films, but he has great talent and will be a good draw in England. His name is Laurence Olivier.'

'Is he good looking?' Lilian giggled.

'We think so. Twenty three and quite tall. It's believed he'll go far.'

'Fine, it will give me a chance to speak English again. What are you going to call the picture?'

'The Temporary Widow. What do you think?'

'Mm … sounds English enough. By the way, is it possible we could find a job for Jens Keith? If you remember he was my choreographer in Vienna and he's now working here in Berlin.'

Richard leant over and took a cigar from a box on his desk. 'My dear Lilian, I would love to, but you know how difficult it's becoming. I'm being pressured by the new Socialist party as to whom I employ. Not only is your friend Jewish but he has, how shall I put it, rather a strange taste in friends.'

'You mean he's got a boyfriend?' Lilian stood up. 'Does that worry you? Lots of people in the theatre have unusual friends.'

Richard sighed and carefully cut his cigar. 'I know my dear, but Herr Hitler is not a man to cross. Now don't take umbrage, I've another surprise for you. I shall hold a party to introduce Laurence to the cast. He's flying in next Thursday and I'll arrange for him to meet you at my house. He can then escort you to the restaurant.'

Lilian knew that this was a chance for Richard to

31

get the most out of the evening as a publicity stunt. For as much as she liked Richard, she suspected he was up to something. She watched him light his cigar carefully. He was a careful man at most things, and certainly not one to cross.

Chapter 3

The years up to 1928 were sowing the seeds of unrest, murder and mayhem. The Workers' Party grew in strength and this was not only demonstrated at the ballot box. Meetings became ugly and after several murders, in September 1928, the KPD (Communists) headquarters were stormed by Goebbels and his men, who exchanged fire with its members.

1929 was the year of the stock market crash on Wall Street. This may have seemed worlds away from life in Berlin, but the German economy was tied in with foreign investment, particularly from America. Now, overnight, the source of money dried up and the scene was set for the Great Depression to spread from America. Adolf Hitler was poised to take advantage of the unrest.

Using his skills as an orator, Hitler, with the support of Goebbels' organising abilities, formulated a hugely successful election campaign in 1930. Mesmerising the poverty stricken population, he won 107 seats in the Reichstag. This was the signal for Nazi storm troopers, be they in civilian clothes or in uniform, to incite crowds to smash the windows of shops and businesses owned by Jews.

***

Richard Eichberg was true to his word. The film *Hocus Pocus* was a huge success when they held their first night in Berlin, followed by a lavish party nearby. With great diplomacy, the director invited the political leaders of the time, including Herr Goebbels of the Nazi party, to join them.

Lilian was escorted to the party by her on-screen romance, Willie Fritsch. The fans were clearly supportive of this fairy tale picture, and after several years of poverty and suppression by the outside world, they went wild with excitement. Willie had his work cut out, gallantly rescuing Lilian from the mob of admirers. Exquisitely gowned and wrapped in a white fur stole, Lilian smiled nervously and waved to the crowd.

Inside the ballroom Richard was waiting and as she entered to great applause, he lifted her hand to his lips.

'Darling, you were wonderful! No, you were sensational, the audience loved you.'

'Thank you, Richard.'

'Now I have someone here who insists on meeting you.' He turned and holding her arm gently moved her towards a rather cadaverous looking man in full evening dress. 'Lilian, may I introduce Doctor Goebbels, the Gauleiter for Berlin?'

The man, taking her hand, bent over it just a little too long for her liking.

'How do you do, Herr Doctor.'

'The honour is all mine dear lady. We hear so much of 'the sweetest girl in the world'. The press comments hardly do you justice!'

Lilian withdrew her hand. 'You are too kind, Herr

Doctor.' Smiling, she moved on to the next person and stopped dead. Facing her was none other than her old dance director, Otto Heinrich. What was more, Otto was in uniform.

'I always knew you would go far.' He smirked and went to kiss her on her cheek, but missed as Lilian stepped back. 'My dear Lilian, be careful, we are now in a position that can make or break even the high and mighty.'

'Otto, why don't you keep that for the street brawls or the chorus lines you're so fond of.'

Otto glared at her. 'What do you mean by that?' he spat.

The tension was broken by a young man in a white tuxedo and black tie who cut across the floor to take Lilian's arm. 'Miss Harvey, may I introduce myself? I'm Guy Parrett, a theatre critic from the New York Tribune. Is it possible you could do an interview for me? The people in America just adore you.'

Lilian regarded the good looking American and smiled. 'A slight exaggeration, I feel. Most of my films have been produced in Germany and those with sound are in German.' She paused for a second. 'Wait, we're about to release an English version of the film you've seen tonight. If you wait until later in the week you may meet the Englishman who is playing opposite me, Laurence Olivier.'

'Super! I look forward to it and don't forget we have a very large population of German patriots in New York.' He smiled and blew a kiss before being swallowed up in the crowd.

The party moved forward to the dining area, where they had a table near the band. Lilian was relieved to see that Otto was not amongst the party, but slightly disturbed to find Dr. Goebbels on one side of her.

However, the evening went with a swing as Lilian danced with a lot of celebrities, including an Austrian count, who was totally infatuated with her. He even went as far as offering Lilian a castle and the accompanying village in return for her favours. Slightly taken aback, she politely turned down his offer and was quite thankful when he returned her to their table. Later that evening, much to the annoyance of the count, Lilian was approached once again by Guy Parrett for a dance. The breach of old fashioned etiquette made the count furious and he had to be admonished by Herr Goebbels, who avoided a scene by threatening the count with two of his henchmen.

Lilian turned to Guy, 'I think you asked me to dance, Mr Parrett?' She took his arm with a little laugh.

'Please call me Guy,' he replied as he started to waltz with her.

'Well Guy, what are you really doing in Germany?'

He smiled down at her. 'The reason for my visit is in my arms.'

'You are either very gallant or extremely forward!'

'Strictly speaking, I am a news correspondent, but sometimes I play truant.'

Lilian laughed. 'And now you are playing truant?'

'Just for this evening.' He looked seriously at her for a moment, then added, 'Tomorrow I'm attending a meeting of the new Socialist party.'

'I see. Do you think it is the future for Germany, Guy?'

Guy paused for a moment as he steered Lilian away from the other dancers. 'I am disturbed by some of their attitudes, particularly Herr Hitler, who has more than a few dangerous viewpoints.'

Lilian glanced nervously around the dance floor.

Guy continued. 'I might add that people like your friend, Jens Keith, should be very cautious.'

'Guy, please be careful. Dr. Goebbels is here and

he is a great admirer of Hitler. You saw earlier what he can do.' She looked up at him. 'How do you know Jens?' she whispered.

'I am what we Americans call nosy,' he replied with a serious note in his voice. At that moment the music came to an end and they stopped dancing. As Guy led Lilian back to her table she nervously changed the subject. 'How do you think our film industry compares with your Hollywood?'

'I can honestly say that you would shine in their company!'

Guy pulled out her chair. Lilian looked up and smiled. 'Mr. Parrett, I do believe you are one big flatterer.'

The following week, Lilian was driven to Richard's residence in the studio's chauffeured limousine. The house was a magnificent villa south west of Berlin, in the suburb of Dahlem. The police were directing the traffic and allowing the guests to be set down at the main entrance where they were ushered through a magnificent hall and ante-room to congregate on the terraces.

'Ah, there you are, my dear Lilian. You're late!' said Richard as he led the way through the crowd of guests on to a terrace, before looking back over his shoulder. 'I have some of the press waiting to meet you and Laurence together.'

'I'm sorry, Richard. The chauffeur had a devil of a time getting in.' Lilian smiled sweetly as he turned to face her.

'Well never mind. Laurence isn't here yet. Now smile for your public.'

'I am smiling!' Lilian replied in a sotto voce voice that hung in the air like icicles, before she swept past him.

The top terrace was crowded with photographers and Lilian quickly realised that Richard had set up a press scrum. For the next ten minutes she was bombarded with questions and flash bulbs.

'Lilian, is there anything between you and this Englishman, Laurence Olivier?'

'Lilian, have you and Willie fallen out?'

'Lilian, are you ever going back to England?'

'Lilian, is it true that you've had an offer from Hollywood?'

'What?' Lilian stared at the speaker. It was Guy.

'I asked if ...' he started to reply.

'Yes I know what you asked, ' Lilian snapped.

But it was too late and she was bombarded with more questions along similar lines.

A shout bought the chaos to some sort of order as Richard appeared on the terrace with his arm around Laurence Olivier's shoulders. Lilian quickly turned his arrival to her advantage and ran lightly across to throw her arms around the English actor.

'Larry! How lovely to see you,' she cried before turning to her host. 'Richard, you didn't warn us that you were going to have a press circus here.' Swivelling back to Laurence she smiled wickedly. 'I told them we were just good friends.'

'Of course, my dear girl. I couldn't wait to see you again.' He kissed her on both cheeks, highlighted by dozens of flash bulbs.

Later that evening as the party was in full swing, much to her dismay, she was confronted by Otto Heinrich; this time he was in civilian clothes, but she noticed he still had that sneer.

'Lilian, we meet again.'

'Herr Heinrich, I didn't know you were so interested in the film business,' she replied coolly.

'My dear young lady, I make it my business to know everyone, particularly as my chief, Herr Goebbels, is taking over the Ministry of Propaganda.' He took Lilian's arm and steered her down the terrace. 'Which reminds me. That American press man, Parrett? He's making some very indiscreet enquiries. It would not be a good move to be associated with someone who seems to have pro-Jewish sympathies.'

'I hardly know the man. As to his friends, it would seem better to have a friend than an enemy. Is that what you socialists want?'

'Well it looks as if you have made another friend. Herr Goebbels would like to have dinner with you next week. Would Tuesday be acceptable?' Otto asked.

'Can't he ask me himself? Or does he always send his lap dog to do his dirty work?' Lilian replied.

'If he didn't think so much of you, I would take steps to see that your days in the limelight are numbered.'

'Are you threatening me?'

'This is the new order of things. We will ensure that the Aryan race regains the superiority it deserves.' Otto's voice rose an octave, attracting the attention of some groups of guests chatting animatedly on the terrace. It was unlikely they heard what Otto was saying over the orchestra that was playing above them, but his mannerisms were obvious. He grasped Lilian's arm with some force, making her wince with pain.   'I think you have a lot to learn …,' then gasped as he was swung round and a punch sent him sprawling.

'I think you have more to learn - to start with, how to treat a lady,' Guy Parrett said with a grim face.

Another voice broke the atmosphere. 'Now, now, what's happening to my leading lady? I cannot allow a jealous feud to spoil the party. Come my darling, Laurence is about to leave and we must not offend our British cousins.' Richard put his arm protectively around Lilian and drew her away. Looking back over his shoulder he glanced at Otto who still lay sprawled on the stone flags of the terrace. 'I should hate to have to report to Herr Doctor that you upset his favourite star.' With that he swept Lilian away into the house.

Otto scrambled to his feet. 'I haven't finished with you,' he snarled at Guy.

Guy regarded the man coldly. 'Oh, I forgot to say, I've sent a copy of my article in the New York Tribune to your boss, saying what a good job I thought he was doing for the German film industry. And we all know how many German ex-patriots there are in my city, who Herr Doctor would love to have as his support.'

Otto stared at the American for a few seconds and then marched away. Guy watched him striding along the terrace and shook his head. 'I can just see him marching in jack boots.'

Chapter 4

In 1931 Erik Charell directed the film for UFA which was to propel Lilian to absolute stardom with her screen romance, Willie Fritsch. One object of the production was to try and break the monopoly of Hollywood in Europe.

Lilian was extremely nervous when she was called into the main offices. A senior executive of UFA ushered her into the boardroom. There were three directors present and the most senior man offered her a chair. He remained standing and glanced around the boardroom table as though he were seeking support. Lilian realised he was more nervous than herself and, because there were three of them present, it was unlikely they would all be there if they were going to fire her. She smiled sweetly at him.

'My dear Lilian, we are planning the first German musical. It will be a lavish production with new music and songs and we would like you to take the lead. But equally important and unknown in the film world, we plan to do separate productions in German, French and English.

Now ... ', he paused, 'we would like you to do all three with different casts!' He beamed at her. 'What do you think?'

Lilian laughed. 'What do I think? You offer me a dream part, no ... three dream parts and ask me what I think. I think I'm dreaming. When do I start?'

'As soon as we finish the casting. Of course Willie will play opposite you in the German version. We'll send you each song as soon as it's ready, so that you can start rehearsing. In some cases they'll be a duet. Now you'd better take some time out for a few days and we'll be in touch. Here's your new contract; we've taken account of the new schedule and it will be tough as we plan to launch the different versions all within a month of each other.'

She took the document she was handed and hardly noticed the congratulations from all the directors as she left the room. In a daze she even passed Willie on the stairs and looked startled when he called to her.

Lilian's enthusiasm reached new heights when, a fortnight later, she received the script together with one of the pieces of music. It was a perfect vehicle for her.

The film was titled *The Congress Dances,* and was

set in Vienna in 1814/15 during the Congress that followed the Napoleonic wars.

Lilian played the part of Christel, a glove seller, who as an advertising stunt threw flowers and her visiting card into the carriages of all the visiting signatories.

One such move attracted the attention of Alexander, the Tsar of Russia. At first she was arrested for what they thought was an assassination attempt on the Tsar, but eventually she was released allowing Alexander, using the business card, to meet the attractive young Christel and fall in love.

The romance was thwarted by Prince Metternich, but it all came to an end when the news broke of Napoleon's escape from Elba and all the heads of state rushed back to their countries. All was not lost for Christel, who fell for Alexander's secretary, Pepi, who stayed behind. Thus it all ended happily thereafter!

Lilian was sitting at the piano one afternoon, trying the song she had been given and using one finger she played the melody.

'You'll never make Carnegie Hall playing like that!'

Startled, Lilian swung round to find Guy standing

in the open French windows. 'Oh my God, you made me jump.' She got up from the piano stool and went over towards him. 'You might have telephoned me and asked if you could come over. I know I said you could call me, but as you can see I'm busy working.'

'What's that in your hand'

Lilian looked guiltily at the wine glass in her hand. 'It helps to lubricate my throat when I'm rehearsing', she replied with a coy smile. 'Would you like one?'

Guy nodded. 'Sure, can I help myself?'

'You usually do!'

'Wow, we are feeling a bit scratchy today.'

Lilian plonked herself down on the large sofa and patted the cushion beside her. 'I need some distraction. This project is driving me mad.' As Guy collected a drink and seated himself next to her, she proceeded to tell him all about the challenge she had.

Guy listened with interest. 'Mm, it does seem quite a tall order, the lead in all three versions. Let's hope it's going to work. Who's backing it?'

'UFA I suppose, although a little birdie told me Paramount had an interest in it.' Lilian paused. 'However, I find that strange, as Herr Hugenburg told me at the meeting that it was a move to strengthen the

German film industry against the might of Hollywood.'

'Well I do hope he's right for your sake. Some of the Hollywood studios are tough opposition. ' Guy took a sip of his drink before changing the subject. 'Now how about dinner tonight? A swanky new Italian restaurant's opened on Friedrichstrasse. Apparently the owner has a cousin with a similar restaurant in New York.'

Lilian smiled. 'How can I refuse, even if you do gatecrash my privacy. Anyway, how did you get into my garden?'

'Your gardener remembered me and likes Lucky Strikes!'

Lilian shook her head and then wagged a finger at Guy. 'But no funny stuff, as you Americans say!'

Guy sighed. 'Oh well, I suppose it will have to be as we say - lady, be good.'

' No, it's you who has to be good … I saw a write-up of that musical and the music is fantastic.'

The restaurant was crowded, Any casual diners were turned away as all the tables were booked. The floor manager recognised Guy as soon as he entered, but when he recognised his pretty escort he nearly choked on his winged collar. 'Why, Miss Harvey, this is an unexpected pleasure, we are honoured,' he grovelled. Without asking if Guy had booked, which he had, he snapped his fingers and led the couple across the floor to a reserved table. Taking the reserved sign off the table he pulled out the chair for Lilian.

To say that their entrance caused a stir was an understatement. A large number of the diners applauded and most of the men stood and acclaimed the actress. Lilian smiled sweetly all round before taking her seat.

'I must remember to mention your name whenever I book a table in future,' murmured Guy.

'Darling, behave or there won't be another time.'

'Touché, I promise to … oh my God, look who just arrived!'

Lilian glanced over her shoulder at the six people who had just come in. 'Who are they?'

'Well the last couple are the American ambassador and his wife. Fred Sackett's a likeable guy, but not a happy man. Rumour has it that he would rather be back in the States working at his family businesses, especially in these lean times. Gee, just our luck, he's spotted us.'

The ambassador steered his wife over to the table

where Lilian and Guy were seated. 'Well I guess I was right, dear. Guy Parrett, you old son of a gun.' He grasped Guy's hand and pumped it up and down vigorously.

'Senator, how are you?'

'That's just it. I wish I was just a Senator. All these charades in Europe are getting me down. The sooner my wife and I get back home the better!'

Having acknowledged the ambassador's wife, Guy introduced them both to Lilian.

'Say, Guy's a dark horse, hiding you away. We've seen several of your films, my wife's a great fan. But Guy always was one for a pretty face!' After the laughter, the ambassador turned back to his fellow-American. 'Seriously, come and see me. We must have a talk.' With that he turned and escorted his wife back to their party.

Nearly a week later, Lilian rang Guy to ask him to dinner. Under instructions to come early, he arrived just after six and was shown into the drawing room where she was seated at a desk.

'Guy, thanks for coming early.' She got up to greet him.

He kissed her on both cheeks. 'This is very intriguing, what's the mystery?'

She walked back to the desk. 'I'm not sure I understand myself but I have been approached by 20th Century Fox to go to Hollywood.' Lilian handed a letter to Guy to read.

'Well, congratulations!' Guy announced, passing the letter back to her.

Lilian walked across to a drinks trolley and poured out two cocktails she had made earlier. 'But why now? Why make the offer when they know I am up to my eyeballs in *The Congress Dances?*'

Accepting the drink, Guy sat down on the sofa. 'I see nothing strange in it. The studio is one of the biggest in the world and you're a top star. Unless...'

'Unless what?'

'Well, you remember we met Fred Sackett the other evening and he asked me to call ... '

Lilian nodded.

'I did go and see him and we had a very long chat.'

'What about?'

'It seems the President is extremely worried about the way things are shaping up in Europe. I've been asked to look at certain aspects over here and your name came up.'

'My God, is nothing sacred!' Lilian finished her drink and got up to walk across to the trolley.

'It seems Anglo-American relations are to be fostered. Your English connections are to be nurtured.'

'Sounds positively obscene.'

'Seriously, the general opinion is that Hitler is itching for a fight and I've been asked to do a little research.'

'You mean spying?'

'Well to put it bluntly …,' Guy replied.

'Yes!' Lilian interrupted.

There was a silence as Lilian picked up the cocktail shaker and brought it over to Guy to top up his glass.

'You didn't have to tell me,' she murmured.

Guy picked out the little stick with a cherry on from his glass and took a sip of the drink. 'I know, but I made one condition.'

Looking puzzled, Lilian took the shaker back to the trolley before returning to the sofa. 'I don't understand, what was it?'

'I would do what they asked, knowing as an

American I have some form of freedom of movement, but you have only got your English nationality and that may not be great protection. I just thought you might wish to consider America.' Guy studied his glass and its contents.

Lilian stared at him. 'Are you proposing?'

Startled, Guy shook his head. 'Er ... no!'

Still staring at Guy it was as if the penny suddenly dropped and Lilian started to laugh. 'Oh you dear boy. Of course, the offer! Somehow you got them to make me a business offer.' She started to laugh again. 'And I thought...'

Guy stood up and walked across to the window. 'Well, if I had thought that you might have said ...' He left the statement unfinished.

Chapter 5

The year 1931 ended on a bad personal note for Hitler. After great success in the elections, with the Nazis becoming the second largest political party in Germany and even allowing for the problems caused by his storm troopers, Hitler's life took a nasty twist.

He rented a small country house in Berchtesgaden. Now aged 39, he settled in and asked his step-sister to take over the running of the household. She duly arrived with her two daughters, Friedl and Geli. The latter was a lively 20-year-old with dark brown hair and Hitler fell hook, line and sinker. However Geli's tendency to flirt enraged Hitler to such a degree that, after one huge argument, he forbade her to leave the house whilst he was away. Finding it all too much, Geli committed suicide. When he heard *the news of her death, Hitler sank into a deep depression.*

He took nearly a year to recover. The eventual turn-around was partly due to his subsequent meeting with the 84-year-old president, Paul von Hindenberg, to present his demands.

From then on, the political infighting began in earnest. The intrigues and bitter personal battles only ended in January 1933, when Hindenburg capitulated and made Hitler Chancellor of all Germany.

***

Days before Hitler was made Chancellor, Lilian accepted what seemed like an attractive contract from 20th Century Fox who had a heavy stake in the German film industry. Thus armed, she amicably ended her association with Richard Eichberg and booked her ticket to the United States.

On the day Lilian climbed the gangplank to the

liner, her chauffeur struggling after her with a hatbox, a vanity case and an overnight case, she was met at the top of the steps by the purser who, well aware of the publicity for the ship's line, made sure that the ship's society photographer was in attendance.

'Miss Harvey, welcome aboard. I hope you enjoy your voyage and if there is anything we can do to make your trip more comfortable, please contact me.'

'Thank you, that's very nice of you.' Lilian smiled graciously at him, before turning and giving the photographers a last minute wave.

'Oh and just one other thing. I do hope you can make the Captain's drinks party, before dinner. You will find your invitation in your cabin.'

'I accept with pleasure.' Lilian replied before following the steward down the gangway.

The Captain's party was a prestigious affair, although not as sought after as a seat at the Captain's table. Lilian had the privilege of receiving an invitation to both.

Dressed in a fabulous dark blue silk gown by Coco Chanel of Paris, Lilian delayed her entrance to great effect and brought a ripple of applause from the other guests.

'My dear Miss Harvey, you look absolutely divine. Your pictures do not do you credit.' The Captain clicked his heels in Germanic style and bent over the actress's hand.

'You are too gallant, Captain.'

'Not at all, I am sure that you will take America by storm and they will take you to heart as we do in our beloved Fatherland.'

'I do hope so, Captain', Lilian paused and then in a quieter voice added, 'do you think the Americans approve of what is going on in our country?'

For a second the Captain looked surprised and then apprehensive before glancing at those nearest to him. 'There are a lot of German settlers in America and I am sure, Miss Harvey, you will be made welcome.'

'Mm… perhaps. I just wondered if they have quite the same viewpoint as some of the people in their homeland.'

'Miss Harvey, I must warn you, I do not get involved in politics and more importantly, you see that dark haired man on the far side of the room talking to the lady in green?'

Lilian, carefully moving to the left of the Captain so that she could see, nodded.

'He's a Nazi, planted here to spy on some of the passengers.'

'You don't approve, Captain?' Lilian asked.

'I don't have an opinion,' he replied emphatically. 'But, it is a warning you should heed. Now I must circulate, so if you would excuse me?'

Lilian spent the next few minutes circulating too. It was rather boring, as all the guests she met asked the same questions, but the tedium vanished when the Captain reappeared and asked if he could escort her in to dinner.

It turned out to be a very enjoyable evening, but as it drew on Lilian began to feel the strain and quietly took her leave. When she was leaving the restaurant a voice behind her asked if she had a nice word for the New York Tribune. She spun round with a smile on her face. 'Guy! What are you doing on board?'

'Hoping to see you!'

'I never know whether to take you seriously.'

'Your friend Otto did. He had me arrested recently when I tried to interview a Jewish banker.'

Lilian put her hand to her mouth. 'Oh no! What happened?'

'Well I managed to get a word to Fred, you remember, our ambassador. He pointed out to that slimeball that it wouldn't look good to the American public if one of their newspaper men was ill treated in Germany by the up and coming Socialist party. They reluctantly agreed and had to let me go. Mind you, not before they got in a few telling punches.'

'I'm afraid that it'll get worse before it gets better,' replied Lilian. 'Speaking of which, take me to the lounge where we won't be overheard.'

They made their way out of the restaurant where people were beginning to settle in for an evening of dancing and general merriment. Selecting a table in the lounge which was fairly discreet, Guy called over the waiter and ordered champagne.

'My, we are extravagant. Just like my husband!'

Guy looked up sharply from his cigarette case he had taken out of his pocket. 'Husband?'

'Don't look so shocked. We are all entitled to a mistake occasionally.'

Guy made a pretence of looking nervously around the lounge. 'He's not with you, is he? I mean, will I suddenly be challenged to a duel by a man twirling a waxed moustache?'

Lilian giggled. 'Hardly. He's coming over next week, when he has finished some business.'

'What does he do?'

'He's a film director. He has work in the States.'

'Which reminds me. What are your plans?' Guy paused as the waiter brought a bottle of champagne in an ice bucket and, making an elaborate flourish, filled the two glasses he had set before them.

They talked and smoked for an hour before Lilian stood up. 'Much as I enjoy your company, I do have to get some beauty sleep.'

'I find that hard to believe. But, hey ho, let me walk you to your cabin.'

'Oh, there's no need ...'

Guy took Lilian's arm and tucking it under his, led her out of the lounge.

It took only a few minutes walk to reach Lilian's cabin, where to Guy's surprise, she had the key in her hand ready. But, as she pushed the door open, there standing just inside the cabin was the dark haired man pointed out by the Captain as a Nazi agent.

Lilian's scream brought her personal steward running down the corridor. At the same time the Nazi pushed Lilian to one side and went to flee the other way down the corridor. Guy managed to catch his arm and spun him round, then kicking his legs from under him he sat on his chest as he went down.

The next morning Lilian and Guy accepted an invitation to the Captain's day cabin.

The Captain ushered them in and, having ensured they were seated comfortably, offered coffee. He walked across the cabin and turned, standing with his hands behind his back. 'I've asked you here this morning because I would prefer to see this unfortunate incident hushed up. I do not approve of these thugs' tactics. It is bad for the shipping line and the world at large. I have been in touch with Berlin and he is to be sent back on the next available ship. In the meantime he is under lock and key.'

The Captain walked back towards his visitors and sat facing them. 'I can only offer my deepest regrets for the whole incident.'

Lilian graciously nodded her thanks.

'However I must warn you Mr. Parrett, the Nazis are determined to keep a close eye on you. They asked a lot of questions; in particular they wanted to know your home address, but I told them you had only registered your office in New York.'

'Thank you, Captain.'

'My friends, this is only the beginning. I fear the worst. If he carries on like this, Adolf Hitler will lead Germany to destruction. Can you imagine what another war will do to us? We are hardly over the horrors of the last one.'

Chapter 6

On January 30th 1933, Hitler was sworn in as the Chancellor of Germany saying - 'I will employ my strength for the welfare of the German people, protect the constitution and laws of the German people, conscientiously discharge the duties imposed upon me, and conduct my affairs of office impartially and with justice to everyone'.

The next step came on the night of February 27th, when the Reichstag was set alight; ironically by a deranged Communist, possibly aided and abetted by Goering's storm troopers. They were to become the notorious and barbaric Gestapo.

After the death of President Hindenburg in August 1934, Hitler combined the post with that of his own as Chancellor. From then on *he would be referred to as the Fuhrer of the German people.*

* * *

Lilian stood at the rails of the liner as it passed the Statue of Liberty. Standing beside her was Kitty Hart, a close friend during her stay in the States.

'Well that's that!' exclaimed Lilian. 'Two wasted years in America. I'm not sorry to leave.'

'Oh, Lilian, it wasn't that bad.'

'It was worse. Let's face it, all I got was a bum load of scripts that were crap!'

Kitty laughed. 'Mm … plus learning a lot of Yankee slang.'

Lilian pouted. 'Yes, well they were.'

'Well I like the free and easy attitude the Americans have.'

'Oh they've got that alright. Especially the men.'

'So I noticed. By the way, how is Mr. Gary Cooper?
You seemed to like his free and easy way.'

'My dear Kitty, he is a very good example of what

I'm talking about.   However, I find I can only take one cowboy a month!'

Laughing, the two turned to watch the Statute of Liberty fading behind them.   Lilian was right in many ways.   The four films in which she had lead parts were not a success; maybe it was her style which was not what the Americans wanted. The age of the sex symbol was beginning and Lilian's style labelled as 'the sweetest girl in the world' was wearing a little thin. Now here she was, returning to Europe via England where she was to film *Invitation to the Waltz,* with two budding stars of the future. Anton Dolin, playing the chief dancer, together with Ronald Shiner taking the part of a street vendor.

Kitty was the first to break their thoughts. 'Talking of American men, isn't that your friend Guy, the American reporter, standing over there talking to that blonde?'

'Where?   Oh Lord, you're right.   Guy Parrett. Pretend we haven't noticed.'

Kitty giggled.   'Too late, he's seen us and is coming over. I must say he is rather good looking.'

'Kitty!'

Guy made his way through the crowd at the rails towards the two ladies. 'Why, hi there Fancy meeting you after all this time.'

'Just fancy!' Lilian greeted him with a definite note of sarcasm. 'Kitty, this is Guy Parrett, one of the Americans I warned you about. Mr. Parrett, my friend Kitty Hart.'

Guy smiled. 'Miss Hart, I hope we shall be the best of buddies!' He raised her hand to his lips.

Kitty laughed. 'A strange chat up line, Mr Parrett.'

'Ah, these Americans are a strange breed,' Lilian added.

Guy turned to her with a huge grin on his face, 'Miss Harvey, I heard you were going back to Germany, but this boat is going to England!'

'Well, well, so it is. Then you must be on the wrong boat.'

Guy smiled. 'Oh no, I have to go to London.'

'What a shame!'

'Miss Harvey, if I didn't know you better, I'd think that you were taking the mickey.'

'Mr Parrett ....'

'Guy, please ...after all we went through together on the boat coming over.'

'Yes... well you took a lot of explaining to my husband,' Lilian replied tartly.

'Just because I told the press we were just good friends.'

'We were!'

'Good, now as friends, how about you two ladies having dinner with me tonight?'

'Oh we'd love to!', replied Kitty enthusiastically.

'Mr Parrett ... sorry ...Guy. We have travelled across the States for the last two days and if you don't mind, perhaps we could take "a rain check" as you Americans say.'

'No problem. I'll meet you both in the lounge bar at six o'clock, tomorrow night. Bye, ladies!' With that Guy turned and left them, leaving Lilian speechless and Kitty with a big smile across her face. The liner's siren hooted derisively after the retreating figure.

The next evening, Guy sat in a comfortable chair in a corner of the lounge bar reading a book, while a pianist tinkled softly on a baby grand in the background. The lounge, which had emptied of its tea drinkers, was slowly filling up with diners looking for their aperitifs. He glanced up and smiled at the two elegant ladies who approached him.

'Ah, there you are. A sight for sore eyes!' He

stood as they took their seats opposite him. 'Now, what would you like to drink - may I suggest a Manhattan cocktail? It is said that in one of the small Frisian Islands it is all the rage, made very popular by some American sailors who introduced it from … Manhattan.'

'Lovely,' enthused Kitty

'Such a mine of information. But I approve of your choice,' added Lilian with a half smile.

'Well, do I detect a thaw in the delectable Miss Harvey?

'Let's just say Kitty talked me into it.'

Guy smiled and beckoned over the waiter. 'What happened to take you back to Germany?'

Lilian regarded him seriously. 'Are you intending to publish this?'

Guy shook his head. 'This is strictly social,' he paused to give the waiter their order.

'Yes, well that's what you said when you intimated we were having an affair on the boat coming over.'

'How divine!' Kitty giggled.

'Kitty! My husband was furious. He threatened me with divorce.'

Passing around his cigarette case, Guy nodded. 'Lilian, you know it would be no great loss.'

Lilian shrugged and pulled a face. 'It was just as bad in the States for him. Being German there was a lot of bad feeling, but now he has a good script he wants me back in Germany.'

'Just be careful. Adolf has kept his Brown Shirts under control, but I think he is planning something big. My editor wants the British slant as we already have Bill Shirer reporting in Berlin. He was at the Nuremberg rally observing the German people who'd applauded Hitler the night before at his hotel, when they looked at him as if he was the next Messiah. At the rally, which was perfectly staged, the audience hung onto his every word, including his proclamation that the German way of life was determined for the next one thousand years.'

Lilian and Kitty sat and stared at Guy. The silence was broken by the waiter who served their drinks.

Guy raised his glass. 'Here's to peace and mud in your eye!'

Kitty raised her glass then stopped. 'You really believe Hitler will take us to war, don't you?'

Lilian frowned at her friend. 'Don't be silly. Guy always does exaggerate things. Cheers!' She lifted her glass and drank half its contents before spluttering and setting it down again. The other two laughed. 'My God, what have they put in that?'

'Five parts rye whiskey to two parts sweet vermouth, a dash of Angostura bitters, stirred on ice and served with a cherry on a stick.'

'You know, you really are the most boring man,' Lilian exclaimed, draining her glass. She giggled. 'Let's have another one.'

'Okay, but then I insist we all go in to dinner. '

Chapter 7

Early in 1935, Adolf Hitler was in his mountain retreat in Bavaria. After some period of time he returned to Berlin to put his latest plan into action. On March 16th he announced to the world that he was reintroducing military conscription. His breaking of the treaty with France and Great Britain was a total affront, but Hitler gambled on them doing nothing. He was right.

***

In England, Lilian finished the film, *Invitation to the Waltz,* which showed her at her best in a genre she was comfortable with. Back in Germany she continued to work with Paul Martin, who was now producing an historical drama. This turned out to be a smash hit with her German fans, probably because, once again, it linked her romantically with Willy Fritsch. It was not her most favourite film, but at least she was in the limelight.

Her next role was more to her liking; it was light and showed off her talent as a dancer and even as a comedienne. One day she was on the set when a visitor arrived.

'Jens, how wonderful see you.' Lilian ran across the stage to greet her old friend. 'What are you doing here?'

'For God's sake, Lilian, are you asking to take a break?' shouted the director as he threw down his file and stood with his hands on his hips.

Lilian looked over her shoulder and called. 'Lunch.' Taking Jens' hand, she led him off the set. They made their way to her dressing room where refreshments were already laid out. Having poured out drinks, Lilian sat down opposite Jens. 'Now then, tell me all. How are you? Have you still got Hans living with you?'

Jens nodded. 'Yes. We're very happy, but we're also very careful. The Gestapo are everywhere, just waiting for a chance to arrest us.'

'Are you working?'

'Well you could call it that. It's a small dance troupe touring Austria, but we're back in Berlin for a week's break and I heard you were filming here.'

'Where are you staying?

'I'm not sure. Hans can't stay with me so he has gone back to stay with his sister in Stuttgart. I thought I might find a reasonable hotel nearby.'

'Rubbish! You must come and stay with us.'

'Us?'

'Paul and me. We got married three years ago. I suppose you might call it a marriage of convenience... he's my director.'

'Ah. What about Willie?'

'Well you may think that Willie has my heart, but you mustn't believe all you read in the press. It's all public relations.' Lilian passed a plate of sandwiches to her friend.

'Thank you. They look delicious and to tell the truth, I'm starving.'

'Oh dear, perhaps we should have gone out to a restaurant.'

'No, nothing like that but Hans, being a dancer, is always on a diet. We choreographers are not quite so demanding.'

They reminisced for another thirty minutes before Lilian stood up. 'I must go back to work. If you return about five, I'll take you to our lodge. Oh, and Jens, be careful on the streets. The Gestapo are a little quieter these days but it doesn't mean they are not dangerous.'

Lilian had a sense of foreboding when she broke the news to Paul about Jens staying.

'You must be bloody mad. You know how dangerous it is to harbour Jews,' Paul paced up and down Lilian's dressing room, 'even worse, do you know what the Gestapo do to homosexual men? They cut off their balls!'

'Paul, don't be so crude.'

'Well don't say I didn't warn you!' retorted her husband and stormed out of the room, slamming the door behind him.

Later that week the Martins had an unexpected visitor. They had just finished dinner and were about to leave the table when the maid came in with a note for Lilian.

'What is it, Clara?'

'A man called on the telephone and asked me to give you this message,' white faced, Clara handed her the note.

Lilian waited until her maid had left the room before she read it. Looking up she stared at Paul. 'Herr

Goebbels is on his way here.'

'My God, where is your friend?'

'Out somewhere. I couldn't stop him and now he could return whilst Goebbels is here.'

'We must remain calm. Get Clara to serve coffee in the drawing room. Assuming Goebbels comes in an official car, we can only hope Jens will see it and have the good sense not to come in.' Paul got up from the table and left the room.

Clara appeared in the doorway. 'Is everything alright, Madam? Shall I clear away?'

Lilian nodded. 'Yes, please. You can serve coffee in the drawing room. We may be joined by visitors, so make sure there is enough coffee.'

'Very good, Madam.' Clara stood whilst Lilian left the room.

It was about half an hour later that a high powered car roared up the drive escorted by two motor cycles. Lilian stifled the urge to move and sat reading a magazine, picking up her coffee and taking a sip.

A few seconds after the front door bell sounded, the drawing door opened and Goebbels brushed brusquely past Clara before she had time to announce him. He was followed by the slimy Otto Heinrich. Both men were in full Gestapo uniform.

Lilian looked up calmly 'Why, my dear Joseph, this is a surprise. I'm afraid you missed dinner, but do join me for coffee.'

'Lilian, this is not a social call...'

'Nonsense. Now what would you like to drink with your coffee? Schnapps?'

Ignoring Otto completely, Lilian got up and walked across to a drinks cabinet. Outwardly she appeared in complete control, but inwardly she shook. It must have been a great performance, because Goebbels looked flustered and came and stood beside her.

'Lilian, I must insist on talking to you.' He spoke quietly.

'Of course ... but..', she glanced pointedly to where Otto was standing by the door.

'Yes ..yes. Heinrich, wait for me in the car.'

'But Herr Reich Minister ...', Otto stammered.

Regaining control of himself, Goebbels shouted 'Out!'

Lilian smiled to herself. She ushered Goebbels to a chair and having poured out a schnapps for him, she sat down opposite, 'Now tell me, what's this all about?'

Goebbels regained his composure and smiled.

'Lilian, you know how difficult it is for me. You are the epitome of young German womanhood and yet because of the state we live in I am torn between my admiration and my sense of duty.'

'My dear Joseph, you flatter me, I am hardly a young woman. Although I am far from being thirty, I feel mature enough to appreciate what you are saying.'

'That's just it. Your friendship with your colleagues must be limited. It has been brought to my attention that Jens Keith is not acceptable as a member of your company.'

Lilian steeled herself from blurting out her immediate reaction. 'Ah… I think Otto has been putting the boot in. At least that is what he would like to do. Ever since I curtailed his amorous advances on a friend of mine, several years ago.'

'I do accept that Otto can be a little over zealous. But, he is only stating the party line.' Goebbels's voice rose an octave.

'Well Jens did come and see me, but it was purely a professional visit. He is a well known choreographer and he was interested in the dance routines we have in my latest film. Where he is now, I have no idea,' Lilian replied, hoping that he would be somewhere far away.

Goebbels finished his schnapps and stood up. 'Is your husband here?'

Lilian shrugged her shoulders. 'Probably. He has a studio and cutting room at the back and buries himself in there more often than not.'

'You are wasted on him. Perhaps I could brighten your life if we have dinner one evening?'

Standing up, Lilian smiled. 'Delightful. Perhaps next week?'

Looking like a cat that had got the cream, Goebbels clicked his heels and in two strides took her proffered hand, raising it to his lips.

It was all Lilian could do - to stop herself throwing up.

Chapter 8

Early on the 7th March 1936, Hitler made his move and three battalions of the Germany Army crossed over into the Rhineland. This was the demilitarized zone, a violation of the Treaty of Versailles. The action was ratified by the German people, with a 98% referendum approval within weeks.

In 1936 Germany staged the Olympic Games and here was Goebbels' great opportunity to excel at what he did best. He decided that it was a great opportunity to promote his country as an elitist power. However, the party enforced their non Aryan rules, thus excluding many of the German athletes. With some exceptions, the Americans included in their 312 competitors nineteen African Americans and five Jews.

To every one's surprise, an openness was displayed in Germany, with all prohibition *notices removed from the areas around the Games.*

***

Guy Parrett was having a bad week. This was the second time he had been rejected for tickets, even applying as a press representative. As he sat in his hotel room, he decided it called for drastic action. Digging deep in his little black book he found what he was looking for and dialled an outside line. The number rang for some time before a voice answered.

'Hello?'

'Hello, may I speak to Miss Lilian Harvey, please.'

'Possibly. Who's speaking?' The voice sounded slightly slurred.

'My name is Guy Parrett.'

'Can I ask what it's about?'

'No... wait, say a friend on her voyage back from the States.'

'Would that be the expert on the cocktail "Manhattan"?'

'Why yes ... '

A giggly female voice floated over the line.

Guy held the receiver away from his face before reconnecting. 'Lilian, is that you?'

'Hello Guy.'

'You sound happy.'

'I should be. I've just finished another film and Paul has left me.'

'He's left you?'

'Well he's away doing another film. But I think he has other interests.'

'I'm sorry.'

Lilian laughed. 'Why be sorry, these things happen and I'm tired of this cat and dog life. Now why are you ringing me?'

'Well to tell the truth, I'm trying to get tickets for the Olympics and I think old sour puss Otto is being a bum.'

'Ah … so it's not my beauty and charm that appeals to you.'

'I am very allergic to, what we say at home, acquiring a "concrete overcoat". Although over here it is probably a Gestapo kiss with a metal bar or some such.'

'I see… okay, seeing it's you, I'll see what I can do. Meet me in the bar at the Hotel Paris tomorrow at twelve; you can buy me a Manhattan and lunch.'

The phone went dead as she rang off.

The next day Guy sat at the bar of the Paris Hotel explaining the intricacies of making a successful Manhattan to the barman. He was just trying to translate why stirring is more important than shaking when his attention was drawn to a figure in the doorway. It was dim enough in the bar, but wearing sun glasses hardly helped Lilian find her date.

He waved to her and she weaved her way carefully through the tables to the bar.

'Lilian...'

Lilian held up her hand before kissing him on both cheeks. 'Sh ... I am trying to be inconspicuous.'

Guy laughed 'I thought it was a hangover.'

'That too.'

'Good. Have a hair of the dog. A Manhattan, that should do the trick,' Guy pushed a full glass along the bar. 'Fritz here, has been practising; he's nearly there. Tell me what you think.'

Taking her glasses off, Lilian climbed on to the stool, thanking her lucky stars that she was wearing a floral tunic dress which reached below the knee; the only problem was that she found it difficult to climb the stool and then stay safely perched. After several attempts she sighed in exasperation and picking up her drink crossed to an empty table.

Smiling, Guy dutifully did the same and was followed by the barman with canapés. 'Fritz, give us ten minutes then bring two more Manhattans and ask the Maitre to bring the luncheon menus.'

'Of course sir.'

Lilian relaxed in the comfortable chair. 'Ah, that's better.' She picked up her drink and took a tentative sip. 'Mm ... delicious.'

'Good. Now tell me, what caused this little slide into melancholia?'

'Oh I don't know. Before he went, Paul and I had a bit of a ding dong regarding Jens. Paul is quite close to Goebbels and he doesn't want to upset the apple cart. So, he takes it out on me. Jens is an old friend and you don't desert your friends in an hour of need.'

'Is it an hour of need?'

Lilian looked around the bar, but there was nobody within earshot. 'I think that after the Games, the Nazis will bring their full force down on all the Jewish people.'

'Can't your friend leave Germany?'

'They are still in Austria but Hans, his friend, has a sister in Stuttgart and visits her often.'

Guy shook his head. 'Lilian, I think you should leave them to their own devices.'

'I guess so.' Lilian finished her drink and picked up her bag. 'Now what was it you wanted? Oh yes, your ticket. My very good friend Joseph Goebbels couldn't do enough for me. Four tickets in the senior party enclosure.' The note of irony was not lost on Guy.

'Oh my God, that doesn't mean I'll have to sit next to Adolf, does it?

'Shh... Now you take two and I'll hold on to the other two. I expect you'll find someone to take.'

Guy pulled a face. 'I was hoping to take you. Ah here come our drinks. Thank you, Fritz. You're a good man.'

Lilian waited until the barman was out of earshot. 'Is his name really Fritz?' she giggled.

'I haven't a clue, but he sure looks like a Fritz!'

'Guy you're terrible. You'd never make a diplomat,' Lilian retorted, following it with a hiccup..

'Diplomat or not, I'm very grateful. Now let's go into lunch before I have to carry you home.'

As it happened, Guy proved a very popular man with his colleagues in the press. He deliberately got those who were blacklisted into the Games unnoticed. On the day of the 100 metres sprint final, he took an English colleague. When they arrived at their seats, who should be next to them but Lilian and her friend Kitty.

Guy greeted them both and introduced his English companion, George Smith, who represented The Daily Express.

Whilst one event was running, Guy took the opportunity to talk to Lilian who was sitting next to him.

'It will be interesting to see if Hitler stays, let alone presents the medal to the winner of the 100 metres dash.'

'Why?'

'Because the odds-on favourite is the black sprinter, Jesse Owens. A magnificent athlete.'

'Have you met him?'

'Sure! A nicer man you couldn't wish for. He comes from a very poor background, his father was a sharecropper.'

Lilian regarded Guy quizzically. 'What's that?'

'It's a poor farmer who, instead of paying the land

owner rent, pays him a percentage of the crops.'

They were suddenly interrupted by a roar from the crowd who greeted the athletes coming on to the track. True to form, the race was won by Jesse Owens in 10.3 seconds, from a fellow American. The winner had a huge ovation, endorsing the public's approval.

Much to Guy's pleasure the two girls joined them for dinner in a fashionable restaurant not far from Lilian's house.

'Did Jesse ever get to shake Hitler's hand?' Lilian looked up from her meal.

'Well he didn't present the medals. But a little bird whispered that he had met him in private. I think he admired him, but it was against his nature to express it in public,' Guy replied. 'What do you think of him, Kitty?'

'Who?'

'Jesse Owens, sleepy! Who did you think I meant, Hitler?'

'I thought he was a magnificent specimen of manhood.'

'Apart from that, you must admit it takes some doing to achieve four gold medals. Our paper gave him two full inside pages in our special edition on the Games.'

George lifted his glass. 'Here's to the greatest athlete of the year.'

They carried on discussing the Games until Lilian hissed. 'Oh my God, don't look now. It's Otto Heinrich and you know how he feels about you, Guy.'

The Gestapo officer was standing inside the restaurant talking to the head waiter, his eyes roaming the room. He suddenly stopped talking as he caught sight of Lilian. He walked across to their table and stood arrogantly with his hands on his hips. 'Well, well, Miss Lilian Harvey, the Jew lover!' he announced in a loud voice.

There was an immediate silence in that part of the restaurant; the proverbial pin didn't drop, but Guy's napkin did. He threw it on the table and stood up, towering at least four inches above the German, and stared down at him.

'That was completely uncalled for. I seem to remember your boss was a little annoyed last time, when he thought you might have upset the good German people in the Lower East side of New York. Now why don't you leave Miss Harvey to eat in peace? After all, it was the Herr Doctor who presented us with tickets for the very excellent Games today. My colleague from

England and I thoroughly enjoyed it.' Guy smiled at the Gestapo officer, 'particularly the hundred metres.'

'Please give our thanks to the kind Doctor,' Lilian added with a sweet smile.

The Gestapo Officer glowered first at Lilian and then Guy. 'I shall not forget this,' he spat, 'and your time will come, American.'

'I thought that for Americans their time came today; you must admit one of them did quite well, old boy,' George interposed innocently.

Chapter 9

At the end of 1937, General Eric Ludendorff died. As one of Germany's senior generals, who belonged to the old school, he would never have accepted Adolf Hitler as his Fuhrer. However, it still left a solid contingent with the old school, so Hitler turned to his dirty tricks brigade.

The first to go was the Commander-in-Chief of the Germany Army, Werner von Blomberg. His young new wife was accused of having been a prostitute. On seeing pornographic pictures of her, produced by Goering, Hitler flew into a rage and sacked Blomberg. The next general to go was Werner von Fritsch, on trumped-up homosexual stories by Himmler.

To prevent a possible coup by army commanders, Hitler promptly got his cabinet to endorse his appointment as head of all the armed forces. This was followed by his next action - to pursue his long desired expansion of Germany's territory.

On March 12th, he engineered the invasion of Austria, a dark day for the 180,000 Jews in Vienna, who were to be purged by the Gestapo in the months to come.

***

Lilian stood in the bay window of her house in Dahlem and regarded the view with little enthusiasm. It was Spring in 1938 and having just finished the film, *Capriccio*, she had nothing in the pipeline and was bored. In the previous year Lilian had purchased a property in Antibes and she now considered spending a month on the Mediterranean. The Italian film director, Augusto Genino, had contacted her and suggested a film he hoped to direct outside Rome. Could they get together and discuss terms? Lilian realised this could be a wonderful opportunity to meet up whilst she was on holiday in the south of France.

Lilian rummaged in her bag and found her address book. Having looked up a number, she dialled it on the phone. 'Kitty, what are you doing for the next few weeks... nothing? That's wonderful. How would you like a holiday in Antibes?' Whatever Kitty's reply was, made Lilian shriek with laughter. 'That can be arranged ... Paul? Oh, he's practically history. He hasn't been home for the past five weeks. He has some little tart in Austria. Look, why don't you ... ' Lilian paused as she watched two large cars, bearing swastika flags, sweeping up the long drive. 'Kitty, I think I have trouble. The Gestapo seem to be invading in force. I'll ring you back.'

There was a persistent ringing on the front doorbell. A minute or so later the drawing room door opened. 'Madam, there are some soldiers here to see you.' Lilian's maid stood in trepidation in the doorway.

'Show them in, Clara.'

The Gestapo officer entered the room and stood to attention in front of her. He clicked his heels and gave a slight bow.

'Miss Lilian Harvey?'

Lilian crossed to a small table and took a cigarette out of a silver box. 'That is my stage name.' She lit the cigarette and waved the officer to a seat.

'I prefer to stand. I have been ordered to ask you to attend an identity parade at the headquarters.'

'What sort of identity parade?'

'I wasn't given a reason.'

'Is it a request or an order?'

'I've been told to use a minimum amount of force. I would be very grateful if you would comply. I'm a great admirer of your films and this does not give me any pleasure.' The Gestapo officer blushed.

'Well, well. A romantic soldier. Whatever will we see next? Give me a few minutes for my maid to get some things and then we'll go and see who it is I have to identify. Not a corpse, I hope?'

'Not as far as I know, Miss Harvey. I will wait in the hall for you.'   The Gestapo officer saluted with raised arm and left the room.

Lilian stubbed out her cigarette and rang for her maid. They spoke quietly for a few minutes, before Clara left the room.   Ten minutes later the Gestapo were watched unseen by the gardener, as they escorted Lilian out of the house. She was bundled into the lead car which drove off at speed down the drive.

The spacious office was furnished with a huge

desk, some chairs and a large sofa.   On the walls were some modern paintings of healthy looking Hitler youth enjoying exercises in sunny fields.   There was one large window overlooking a bare courtyard with a high wall on the ground floor just below.   The Gestapo officer who escorted her in offered Lilian a chair and followed it up by proffering a cigarette from his own, very elegant, silver case.

'I do apologise for this inconvenience, Miss Harvey. I am under orders, which you may understand I have to obey.'

Lilian nodded. 'Of course Leutnant.   Have you been in the ... army long?'

'Ten months.   I had intended to teach, but my father who is a semi-retired General insisted I did my stint. For the Fatherland, of course.'

'Of course!' Lilian recognised the irony in his voice.

Their conversation was interrupted by the door being flung open and the figure of Otto Heinrich striding in.   He stopped by Lilian and rudely snatched the cigarette from her fingers, stubbing it out violently in an ashtray.

'Herr Sturmbannfurer, there is no need ... Miss

Harvey has been most co-operative ...,' the Leutnant looked shocked.

'Get out,' the Sturmbannfurer rounded on his subordinate. 'Get out!' His voice screamed the last command.

With troubled face the junior officer clicked his heels and left the room.

Otto went round to his chair behind the desk and sat contemplating the woman before him. After a few moments he picked up a file on his desk. Opening it he carefully turned the sheets inside. 'I have had a very difficult day. One man in particular is being most uncooperative. He refuses to answer my questions.' Pausing, he looked down at the file. His last few words were spoken in an almost silky whisper. 'The reason I have asked you here, is to persuade him to tell me what I want to know.'

Recovering from her shock at Otto's confrontation, Lilian shook her head. 'Herr Heinrich, I have no idea who you are talking about.'

Otto reached under his desk and pressed a bell push. The door opened and a private soldier stood at attention in the doorway. 'Sir'.

'Bring him in,' he barked.

'Sir,' the private soldier left, shutting the door behind him.

For a minute or two Otto ignored Lilian and continued to read the contents of the file. There was a knock on the door and he casually looked up. 'Come in!'

The door was pushed open and a man was dragged in by two men dressed in Gestapo uniform. His face was covered in blood and he groaned as they dumped him on the floor.

'No, no, no!, put him in a chair. How do you expect him to have a conversation with Miss Harvey, whilst lying on the floor?'

The two soldiers lifted the man onto the chair offered by Otto. Lilian looked on in horror with a hand over her mouth as the prisoner slumped forward with his head on his chest.

Otto strode over and yanked the man's head up by his hair. 'Well?'

Lilian sobbed as she recognised the battered face. It dawned on her that the man was Hans, the friend of Jens. He was hardly conscious, but he seemed to recognise Lilian, for he shook his head in a warning. It hurt him to do so and he groaned and closed his eyes.

'Oh, Hans, what have they done to you?'

'Good. Now we are getting somewhere. At least you recognise him.' Otto smirked. 'Now we come to the reason I asked you here.'

'How could you do this?'

'What?'

'How could you do this horrible thing?'

'Simple. All I need is the present address of this pervert's friend. I think you know the friend, Jens Keith?'

'If you think I would betray my friends ...'

Spinning on his heels, Otto reached across to his desk and picked up a rubber truncheon. Lilian felt sick as he brought it down on one of Han's wrists. The man screamed and passing out, slid from the chair.

Lilian started forward but stopped as Otto turned back and brought the truncheon hard down on the desk in front of Lilian. 'I will have the answer!' he screamed at her, emphasizing each word by beating time with the truncheon on the desk.

Chapter 10

Otto appeared to be completely out of control and for the first time Lilian feared for her own safety. Between his rants he continued to strike his desk with the cosh. After a while he reached over to the bell and summoned his aides. They appeared promptly and dragged the unfortunate Hans out of the room.

Otto watched in silence before perching himself on the corner of his desk in front of Lilian. His mood seemed to have swung again as he calmly spoke to her. 'Now I will only explain this once. If you do not tell me the whereabouts of this Jew, Jens Keith, I'm afraid that it will be worse for his perverted friend.'

Lilian summoned up her courage and looked Otto in the eye. 'I will never give you the satisfaction. Ever since I've known you, I realised you are a sick bully. You prey on weaker people who cannot fight back. I can't believe that Herr Goebbels knows you have me here, let alone what you are doing to that poor man.'

'I am perfectly entitled, in my capacity of Sturmbannfurer in the Fuhrer's esteemed Gestapo, to act accordingly.' His voice rose. 'We Ayrians will stamp out all accursed money-grabbing Jews who contaminate German society.'

Lilian shook her head. 'If you've finished I would now like to return home,' she replied coolly.

Otto rose from the table and strode over to the door. Opening it, he stepped out of sight and Lilian could hear him speaking to someone in the next room. She tried to hear what he said, but it was too muffled. Seconds later he returned, 'As you are unwilling to help us in our enquiries I am forced to demonstrate the consequences.' He strode across the floor and taking her arm forced her over to the window. 'Now watch!'

Lilian looked out onto the deserted courtyard, which suddenly erupted into life. A file of soldiers armed with rifles marched into view followed by two other soldiers who half dragged Hans across the cobblestones. They reached the wall, where they tied him to two iron rings.

A junior Gestapo officer lined up the soldiers, who faced the prisoner. He briefly glanced up at the window, where Otto stood watching.

He nodded his head. There was a sharp order to take aim. Lilian closed her eyes as a volley of rifle fire was heard and without looking at the result she slumped to the floor in a dead faint.

Guy was in the middle of a report for his New York editor when a personal call was put through to his desk. 'Yeah? Yeah, put her through … Hi Kitty, how are you?'

Slowly he got to his feet and with an ashen face he continued his conversation. 'What! Are you sure? … Okay, leave it with me.' He rang off and sat down heavily. For several moments he was deep in thought. Finally he picked up the phone. 'Jane, get me the Ministry of Propaganda, say we would like to speak to their press officer on a matter of diplomatic relations.' He put down the phone and lit a cigarette.

The phone buzzed and Guy picked it up. 'Hi, this is Guy Parrett of the New York Tribune, who am I speaking to, please?'

There was a long pause. 'Gee, well that's too bad. You might tell him I am filing my copy for tonight's edition and I have it on good authority that the Gestapo are holding one of Germany's - no the world's - favourite actresses. I am sure the German Americans in the States will be appalled at the way Herr Goebbels lets his minions treat the elite of the film world. Especially women.' Guy grinned and held the phone away from his ear. The copy writer sitting opposite raised his eyebrows. 'Wow!'

It took Lilian several minutes to recover from her collapse; she found herself being lifted by the two Nazi soldiers and placed upon the sofa on the far side of the office. Otto was not in the room. She closed her eyes and tried to shut out the horrid scene, but it wouldn't go away. After several minutes the door opened abruptly and Otto strode back in, going round behind his desk.

'Let that be a lesson to you. I've warned you many times that we are not a force to be trifled with. Now you will tell me where to find this man!'

Lilian, with some effort, swung her feet on to the floor. 'And I've told you that I can never betray good friends.'

'Then we shall have to call on another one of your so called friends and ask her. I believe Kitty Hart is in your confidence?'

'You bastard, I shall ...' Lilian's protest was interrupted by one of Otto's phones.'

Snatching up the receiver Otto barked 'Yes?'. His demeanour changed in seconds. 'Sir, no sir. No, I mean yes, sir ...' Standing up and to attention, he stammered his replies with a flushed face. Otto finally clicked his heels and slowly put the phone down. Without another glance at Lilian he rang the bell on his desk for his aide. The Leutnant, with two soldiers, appeared immediately. 'Miss Harvey is going home, find her a car!' Gathering his cap and cane he hurried from the room.

Chapter 11

The two women sat in the weak spring sunshine on the terrace of Lilian's home. It was late morning and Clara, her maid, arrived with a tray of coffee and pastries.

'Oh goody. I love these Danish pastries.' Kitty paused and put her hand to her mouth. 'Oh Lilian … I'm so sorry, I'd forgotten Jens is Danish. That was most thoughtless of me.'

Lilian smiled wanly. 'Kitty you can't hide from the truth. We're amongst a load of murderers. They'll try and find Jens, but I will not give him away. The sooner he can get out of this terrible country, the better.'

'What did Herr Goebbels say to you?'

'He didn't. He sent round a note. Not an apology, mark you!'

'Well thank goodness he did intervene. I couldn't think of anything else to do, so I contacted Guy.' Kitty took a cup of coffee from her friend and then smiled in delight as she accepted a pastry.

Lilian smiled back at Kitty. 'I don't know how you stay so slim.'

Kitty ignored the comment. 'Do continue with

what happened.'

'Well there's nothing to tell, really. Guy phoned me last night to make sure I was home safely. But he refused to talk about it on the phone. Now let's change the subject.' She paused to sip her coffee. 'You said you could easily get away for a week or two.'

Kitty nodded with her mouth full.

'In that case, suppose we leave the day after tomorrow. I've telephoned the caretaker in Antibes and she will open up and air everything. She's marvellous. Fresh food will be there waiting for us. By the weekend we can be swimming in the sea!'

Half choking, Kitty spluttered a reply. 'You must be joking, the Med is freezing in late May.'

'Don't be such a spoilsport. Besides, I bet you'll want to swim, when you learn that Guy is driving us down.'

Kitty shrieked. 'How absolutely delightful!'

'I thought you might be pleased.'

'I'm not treading on anybody's toes, am I?' Kitty glanced at Lilian before she took another bite of her pastry.

'Certainly not,' Lilian emphatically replied. 'Now let's make some plans. If you like, you can come over for dinner tomorrow night, bring your luggage and stay the night. Then we can be off at eight o'clock sharp. Guy said he'll be here at seven.'

'One day to pack! What on earth should I take?'

'Nothing too formal. We can eat out on some days. There are delightful restaurants nearby.'

Kitty smiled, 'Sounds idyllic, as long as I don't put on too much weight. Two weeks with you and I shall be the size of a house. Anyway, what made you buy the house in Antibes in the first place?'

Lilian looked thoughtful for a minute. 'Several reasons really. I was getting a little perturbed about my future here and I do like the climate in the south of France. Also, it was an investment, I couldn't trust Paul, which proved right enough.' She paused to finish her coffee. 'Besides, men can be such bastards.'

'What about Guy?'

Lilian glanced at her companion. 'What about him?'

'Well, I always thought you two would hit it off.'

Lilian looked wistful. 'He's been married, you know,' she paused, 'two children.'

'Well?'

'I think he's scared of a full commitment. He's

married to his job and although I'm very fond of him, there's no spark.'

'Have you ever slept with him?'

'No comment!'

'Whenever anyone says that, they are …'

'Gosh, is that the time? I promised to ring Augusto Genina at twelve.' Lilian finished her coffee.

Smiling, Kitty finished her second pastry and drained her coffee, before standing up. 'That was lovely. What time tomorrow night?'

'Shall we say seven?'

'Fine. Then you can tell me when you slept with him!'

Lilian laughed.

The large Mercedes saloon drove up the drive of Lilian's villa in Dahlem. It was early and there were few people about in the suburbs of Berlin. The dew was still on the grass and there was a nip in the air. The driver's door opened and a man in a chauffeur's cap and overcoat, with collar turned up, eased himself out of the driver's seat. Stretching, he made his way over to the front door and rang the bellpull that hung from an iron bracket on the wall. He waited for a while and at first there was no reply, so he rang again. Suddenly an upstairs window was thrown open. The man stepped back and looking up called out. 'Your car awaits, madam.'

'Guy!'

'Sh …' The man held his finger to his lips.

'Do you know what time it is?'

'I know, but let me in.'

A few minutes later Lilian, wrapped in a dressing gown, opened the door. 'For God's sake, Guy. I said we would leave at eight. It's half past six!' She moved aside to let him in and he closed the front door. 'Honestly, you have no …'

Guy silenced her with a kiss. 'I know. Find me some hot coffee and I'll explain.'

'Well you'll have to make it yourself. Clara's not up yet and I haven't had a bath or done my make-up and …'

'You look wonderful,' Guy interrupted her. 'Now show me the way to the kitchen.'

An hour later Lilian appeared in the kitchen where Guy was teaching Clara to cook her eggs 'sunny side up'.

'Guy, are you upsetting Clara?'

'Oh no, madam, Herr Parrett is teaching me how to cook eggs, fried American style.'

'I wondered what smelt, but we'll eat in here, Clara. Kitty will be down in a minute. Now come and sit down, Guy.' Lilian sat down at the large kitchen table and poured herself some coffee.

Guy picked up his coffee and joined Lilian at the table. 'I'm sorry about this, but I had to give some obnoxious little man the slip. He's been following me for days, ever since you escaped the clutches of Otto the 'Orrible!'

'They are getting worse. They're determined to find Jens, but he's gone to ground and I don't know ...' Any further thoughts of Lilian's about Jens were dismissed by the arrival of Kitty looking quite glamorous.

'Guy, how wonderful,' she shrieked.

'Good morning, Kitty, I say, you look a sight for sore eyes!' Guy smiled at Lilian over Kitty's shoulder as she embraced him; the response was a most unladylike protrusion of the tongue from Lilian.

Disentangling himself, Guy sat down again and raised his coffee cup. 'Here's to a peaceful holiday!'

Chapter 12

The trip to Antibes was a great success; with a film planned in Rome for later that year, the break was more restful than Lilian could imagine and she found the nightmare of Hans' death receding a little each day.

One evening she threw a party for friends and neighbours. The tension of the last few weeks soon evaporated. The day had been warm and late in the evening several of the guests swam in the pool.

Kitty appeared in a fetching two piece swimsuit. Laughing, she pirouetted in front of Guy. 'What do you think?'

'Think! I'm stunned! I must say it suits you.' He watched as she dived into the pool. Surfacing she clutched her halter neck and let out another peal of laughter.

'She's been dying to show you, ever since she bought it.' Lilian stood with a wry smile.

'I did hear that Busby Berkely introduced them in his latest film, *Footlights Parade*, but I didn't realise how revealing they really can be.' Guy replied.

'Perhaps you should join her before one of my

neighbours makes an embarrassing move.'

'Is that likely?'

'Well, several of them look a little over-heated!'

'Give me two minutes.' Guy disappeared into the house and true to his word two minutes later emerged in a costume. He dived towards Kitty who swam towards him. As he surfaced she wrapped her arms around him.

'My hero, you saved me!'

'From what? You certainly weren't drowning.'

Kitty giggled. 'A fate worse than that!'

'Oh you mean losing the top of your swimming costume.'

'Would you mind?'

'I'm sure I would be enthralled.'

'Liar!' She pulled Guy towards her and for a brief moment he was aware of her warm body against his as she kissed him before turning away to swim up the pool.

Their stay in Antibes continued to be a happy one although Guy was puzzled by Lilian's indifference to Kitty's obvious flirtation. In some ways she positively encouraged it. Too quickly their time in the south of France came to an end and they prepared themselves for their return to Germany.

Guy took no chances though, when driving the two ladies back to Germany. Prior to their arriving back in Berlin he donned the chauffeur's uniform once again.

The streets were full of soldiers stopping people and asking for their papers. At one point, they passed some uniformed men kicking a man who was lying curled in a ball on the pavement.

'Oh God, look at that poor man!' cried Kitty.

'Don't look at them. They are no better than wild animals,' replied Lilian.

Slightly further on where there were fewer people, Guy pulled the car over and went into a shop to purchase a newspaper.

'What are the headlines?' Lilian leant over from the back seat.

'Apparently it's now Czechoslavakia's turn. This man is a true megalomaniac. I must get back to the office and see what the situation is. If it goes much further I can't see Great Britain standing by and letting him invade the Sudetenland.' He passed the paper over to Lilian and turning back started the car.

'Perhaps we should go back to Antibes?' Kitty suggested tentatively.

'If we do, I could lose all my German investments if there is a war,' Lilian retorted.

'Well, let me get you home first,' replied Guy, adding, 'and try to keep your heads down.'

'Yes. Especially if that revolting man, Otto, is about,' murmured Kitty.

Lilian used the next few days to sort out her affairs and discreetly put some of the property she owned on the market, making it known that she was investing in a holiday home.

It was late July when Lilian received a phone call. The male voice was familiar as he announced that he had a script ready for her. Puzzled, Lilian asked which film he was referring to and was told *The Ronacher Meeting*. At the mention of the Viennese theatre the penny dropped.

'Oh yes … how are you? Before she could say anything else the voice interrupted her.

'When would you like to read it?'

Slightly flustered as at last she recognised Jens' voice, Lilian stuttered a reply. 'Well … if you could send a courier over late this morning, I'll try and read it before the weekend.'

Putting down the phone, Lilian walked upstairs

and looked down the drive to the road. A large black saloon had parked about thirty yards from her drive entrance. She thought for a minute and then referring to her phone book dialled a number. 'Guy, can you get over here straight away? I would like to discuss a proposition for a film with you.'

'Ah,' there was a pregnant pause and a deep sigh before he added, 'I suppose so, but I must be back in the office by lunch time.'

At about half past eleven a motorbike came up the drive. The rider wore a leather coat, cap and goggles. Over his shoulder he carried a bag often worn by dispatch riders. Taking off his gloves he took out a pad and studied it for a moment before tugging on the iron bell pull. The occupants of the black saloon watched as the front door was answered by Clara who let the rider into the house. He carried the bag into the reception room where Lilian was waiting with Guy. She threw her arms around the visitor and led him to the sofa where she sat holding Jens' hands.

'I am so sorry about Hans. It was terrible.'

He nodded. 'I heard what happened. One of the cleaners in the building gives us information. It is getting much worse. Whole families are leaving, people just disappear without trace.'

'What will you do?'

'I would like to go to Switzerland, but I am told they are looking for me on the border. I could try using the motorbike again, as we aren't allowed cars any more. By the way, that was a great idea, but Guy, are you sure that you can ride a motorbike?

'Of course.'

Lilian nodded. 'Don't worry about Guy, he's old enough to look after himself.'

Ten minutes later a rider left the house and roared off down the drive, past the black limousine with the two Gestapo passengers, who idly watched him go past, with little interest

Jens gave a rare smile. 'I would have tried to use the bike to get out, but I doubt whether I could go very far. They check most vehicles going out of the city.'

'We must think of another way.'

'Lilian, I've put you in enough danger already. It must have been terrible for you.'

'Mm … If Goebbels hadn't intervened, I hate to think what my fate would have been.' She thought for a moment. 'Of course we could use Guy again. He chauffeured us last time and we got away with it. If we could smuggle you out of Berlin perhaps we could take the road south west and get you into Switzerland through France. I've heard that there are a lot of German spies in France, but mostly in Paris. We could be going to my house in Antibes and I do have a film to make in Italy.'

Jens smiled again. 'How exciting. What's it called, who's the director and more importantly, who's your male lead?'

'Oh, it's called *Castles in the Air* and directed by Augusto Genina. He won the Mussolini Cup a couple of years ago.'

'He's good. What about the male lead?'

'Vittorio De Sica. An adorable man, but a little old perhaps.'

Jens got up and walked to the window which looked out on to the terrace at the back of the house. 'You realise that if they discover you have helped me escape, they will show no mercy. My cousin was shot for trying to help an old man those Nazi thugs had beaten up in the street.'

Lilian nodded. 'I'd like to go to Paris after the film in Rome. I've been offered a part in a French translation of one of my films. However, I still have a commitment for another film opposite Willie here in Berlin early next year. But first we must get you out of Berlin, preferably at the same time I go to Rome. Now this is what I thought we could do.'

In the end it was quite simple. Lilian threw a large, lavish party and invited her director, Richard, several friends in the film business and to everybody's surprise, Herr Joseph Goebbels.

It was a sumptuous formal dress affair and the ladies, mostly actresses, were in the latest backless dresses from Paris. Lilian had arranged to have the guests ushered through to the terrace where a quintet played quietly, as the guests mingled whilst sipping champagne and accepting canapés from a bevy of young waitresses.

'If I didn't know you better I would say that you are setting the stage for a charade,' murmured Richard as he paused behind her.

Lilian laughed. 'My dear Richard! Why would I do that?'

'Primarily because you can't stand Goebbels and also that American friend of yours is conspicuous by his absence.'

Lilian glanced briefly across the heads of the throng, where Goebbels was leaning towards a young actress who was wearing an unfashionably low cut dress.

'Perhaps it's called survival, Richard.'

'Whatever. Take care!' He moved on to join a writer who was besieging one of his young producers.

'My dear Lilian, what's this I hear?'

Lilian turned to find her screen lover, Willie Fritsch, standing in front of her with hands on hips.

Lilian regarded him with amusement. 'Oh hello, Willie. I don't know. What is it you've heard?'

'A little bird told me you are leaving our beautiful Fatherland, to make films for that horrible man in Rome.'

'Oh dear, didn't he offer you a part?'

Willie glowered and beckoned to one of the waitresses for canapés. Choosing one with exaggerated care, he turned back to Lilian. 'I hear you have been to Antibes for a holiday with that American.'

'Oh, you mean Guy? I think Kitty is smitten and she insisted he came with us. And, by the by, we are going back again next month for a short holiday before I start filming.'

'Well just make sure you are back in time to make *Frau am Steur,*' he retorted.

Lilian smiled as Willie beat a hasty retreat before she could reply. The smile broadened as she watched him pause by Goebbels and enter into conversation. They glanced in her direction several times; the plan was working.

Chapter 13

Lilian and Kitty sat in the back of the Mercedes limousine outside Frankfurt railway station. The clock on the front of the main hall showed it was just past eleven o'clock. The plaza in front of the station was quiet and the occupants of the car had a good view of the entrance. As another train arrival caused people to spill out of the station, the chauffeur in the Mercedes got out and stood by the car. Presently a man detached himself from the throng leaving the station. He walked across to the vehicle and the chauffeur opened the rear door for him to get in.

As they sped down the road Lilian clapped her hands in delight. 'Well done, everyone!'

'We're not through the border yet,' commented Guy as he struggled out of his coat.

'Ah, we thought of that,' Kitty intervened. 'The idea is to drop Jens off at a village not far from the border, where he will be met by a farmer friend. They will then use a minor border crossing that rarely checks people leaving, especially any with animals. You can then take over as chauffeur and drive on to pick Jens up in Scheibenhard, the part of the village which is across the German border in France, giving us time for lunch in Strasbourg.'

'Sounds good to me,' replied Guy, adding, 'I haven't had a bite to eat since six o'clock this morning and I'm starving.'

The lunch was taken in one of the older hotels in the city, as they had decided not to draw attention to themselves. After lunch it was a straightforward run to the Swiss border near Lausanne. Jens insisted on driving again; as he pointed out, Guy would have enough to do to reach Antibes that night. Just before the border they said their farewells and Jens promised a tearful Lilian to keep in touch.

Luckily the large Mercedes ate up the kilometres and they eventually arrived at the Villa Asmodée in the French resort just before eight that evening. The housekeeper had left cold meats and salad, which they took out to the table on the patio.

The air was warm and the scent from the purple and pink oleanders was heady. In spite of their success it started as a subdued meal, until Lilian produced two bottles of local rosé, which had been left in the bottom of the fridge. Guy lifted his glass. 'Here's mud in your eye!'

The others raised their glasses and as one, toasted Jens.

Lilian had a call from Jens the next day. Firstly to thank her and say he had arrived at his friend's house without incident. But secondly, to say that he had escaped just in time. The Gestapo had raided the house where he had been living on the outskirts of Berlin. The people there had no idea that Jens had left and believed he was visiting someone on the other side of the city. It was only after she rang off that Lilian wondered if whoever had raided the house knew that she was friends with Jens and would start looking for her.

Nothing more was heard, and a week later Lilian and Kitty drove down to Rome to start filming. The weather was glorious. Using the Lagonda Rapier that Lilian had bought on her last trip to England, they took the picturesque coast road to Pisa and then turned off to Florence. Here they spent two days savouring the delights of Italian cuisine as well as some serious shopping.

It was while they were in Rome that Lilian got a call from Guy. He'd returned to Berlin via London.

'Hi Lilian, old thing!'

'Guy, not so much of the old thing. I do wish you would drop some of those awful colloquialisms.'

A hoot of laughter came down the line. 'How's the filming?'

'Good. Kitty has a part, too, which she is very pleased about, especially as I had to work hard to persuade her to come.'

'Are they looking after you?'

'Certainly; the Italian men are delightful and they have such small arses!'

'Trust you to notice their asses.'

'Arse, darling! Ass is something you ride.'

'There's no accounting for taste!'

'Guy! Now why did you ring me?

'When I was in London I met up with an old friend. He told me that shortly there will be a conference in Munich and moreover, that Chamberlain had agreed to go. But the most worrying thing is - it is thought Hitler is preparing to occupy the Sudetenland. If it is accepted, we think he'll not stop there. I believe that war is inevitable, if so, you should stay in France.'

'Don't be silly, Guy. Anyway, I shall stay down here for Christmas. Why don't you join us?'

'Subject to the whim of my editor, I'd love to.'

'Fine. Now you be a good boy and I'll see you in December.'

'You too, and love to Kitty.'

Lilian put the phone down and sat for a moment in deep thought. She needed to move more of her assets out of Germany.

Chapter 14

On September 15th 1938, Neville Chamberlain flew to meet Adolf Hitler, who demanded the transfer of the Sudetenland, complaining that the Czechoslovakians were persecuting the Germans who lived there.

On the 23rd the British Prime Minister returned to Germany and agreed to Hitler's terms. But Hitler refused to abide by them and stated his intention to take over the whole of Czechoslovakia, having planned to carve the country up between Germany, Poland and Hungary, unbeknown to Chamberlain.

This time Hitler realised he might have gone too far. The German people did not enthuse about the prospects of another war and at a final meeting with the British and French prime ministers, he agreed just to occupy the Sudetenland.

Winston Churchill castigated his government, calling the Munich Agreement 'a total and unmitigated defeat'.

Having met his first objective, Hitler now began what was known in future as the Holocaust; the complete extermination of the Jews. On the so called Night of Broken Glass, at least 17,000 Jewish people, including women and children, were forcibly taken and left on the Polish border. Rejected by the Polish government they were virtually stateless and homeless.

***

The phone rang in Lilian's hotel room just as she returned from dinner. Sighing, she picked up the receiver. 'Yes?'

'Hi, Lilian.'

'Guy, is that you? Do you know what time it is?'

'Gee, I do love it when you talk dirty to me!'

'Seriously, I have to be at work at seven for

make-up. I do need my beauty sleep these days. Now what do you want?'

'Last night they transported thousands of Jewish people out of Germany to the Polish border. They rounded up whole families including the family Jens had lived with and they also found out he had escaped to Switzerland. And then found evidence of your involvement during the search of the house.'

'Guy, how did that happen? Jens was so careful. There is no way he would leave anything lying around.'

'I don't know. A letter or postcard? Whatever, be on your guard. There is one person who would take great delight in your arrest.'

'We've got two more weeks of filming and then I shall be back in Antibes. I'll be safe there.'

'Be careful where you are. It appears that Mussolini was in on this so called deal they did with the British Prime Minister, Chamberlain. The Gestapo have their contacts in Italy.'

'I promise to be careful, Guy... and thank you for the warning. I'll see you in a fortnight or so.'

'Okay babe!' The phone went dead just as a knock came at the door, making Lilian nervously drop the receiver. She opened the door to Kitty.

'My God, you look awful!' Kitty exclaimed as she carried some bottles of water into the room.

'Thanks!' Lilian repeated Guy's message. 'And by the way, Guy's coming down for Christmas.'

Kitty gave a quiet squeak of delight.

Three weeks later Lilian and Kitty were on their way back to France. Autumn had truly set in and with the hood up on the car, Lilian carefully negotiated the coast road along the Italian Riviera, which was comparatively quiet. It was when they got to the frontier that reality set in. There were the usual customs officers, but behind them the roads were crowded with tanks and soldiers fully armed.

Lilian handed over her passport showing her British nationality. What with that and the English Lagonda, the customs officer hardly took a second glance at her. But on examining Kitty's passport he peered past Lilian to take a second look at the woman seated in the passenger seat.

'Un moment, Mademoiselle.' He disappeared into the customs building and returned with what appeared to be his senior. They went round to the passenger side as Kitty wound down her window.

'Would you step out of the car, please?' The senior man politely opened the car door.

Nervously, Kitty complied with his request. 'Is there something wrong?' she stammered.

'Why are you coming to France from Italy? Have you come from Germany first?' The tone of his voice was unforgiving.

'I and my friend have been making a film in Rome,' replied Kitty.

'Oh, and would I know you or your friend?' the Customs officer commented sarcastically.

Because the low slung sports car had a hood, the man was unable to see the other occupant of the car and, as if on cue, Lilian opened her door and stepped out, drawing herself up to her full height of five foot one inch. As always, Lilian dressed for her public and the effect on the older senior man was electric. Recognising the actress from the French versions of her films, he even had the grace to blush.

'Miss Harvey, I do apologise, I didn't see you there,' he spread his hands as if explaining how low the car was. 'I apologise to you, too.' He produced a small bow of his head to Kitty. 'We are a little nervous of things at the moment, as you can see.' He continued his gesticulations, this time at the military presence.

Lilian smiled sweetly. 'I do understand. It's not a good time in Germany too and you are quite right to be careful.'

'Thank you for being so understanding.' The man turned to the guards manning the barrier and waved it up. 'Bon chance, madame!'

Kitty and Lilian got back in the car and threaded their way through the military vehicles to continue towards Nice.

'Phew, they are touchy. I think Guy must be right. He did say that he thought war could be inevitable.' Lilian sounded her horn as a local farmer started to drive across the road in his old lorry, loaded with sheep.

'It'll be terrible,' replied Kitty, 'it was bad enough in the Great War. I lost so many of my relatives.'

'There's no use worrying about it. Let us enjoy the next few weeks and then in the New Year we'll decide what to do next. Besides we have Christmas to look forward to and Guy is coming down. We'll have a great party!'

'Mm, sounds interesting!'

Lilian glanced quickly across at Kitty and laughed.

Changing gear to take the next corner, she murmured, 'Poor man!'

Chapter 15

The villa had a desolate look about it; even the oleander around the balcony looked tired. The Christmas decorations had been taken down and now some friends, who had been staying, were leaving in their car. A taxi made its way up the drive and stopped by Lilian. Turning towards the house she called out Kitty's name. Her guests' car made its way down the drive just as Kitty emerged from the house, followed by Anton, the gardener, who was struggling with two enormous suitcases.

'I am sure I didn't bring half as much luggage when we came,' she moaned.

'Darling, it was all the shopping you did in Italy.'

'Well if I hadn't, I could have taken a flight from Nice and been in Berlin in a couple of hours.'

'Don't moan. Anyway you can sleep on the train, or you never know, you might meet a handsome prince who will whisk you off to somewhere exotic.'

Kitty laughed. 'Yes and he will probably be fat and bald, just like that Count who wanted to whisk you off into his castle and have his wicked way with you.'

Lilian gave an exaggerated shudder. 'Ugh, don't remind me.' She pulled her coat tight around her before she embraced Kitty, promising to meet up later in the month.   As the taxi drove off, the maid came to the door and called Lilian to the telephone.

'Hello?'

'Lilian, it's Paul.'

'Paul. How are you?' she replied coolly.

'Lilian, you remember I said that I had another part for you? Well we want to start shooting before the spring. It's called *Frau am Steuer*.'

'Woman at the Wheel! I don't know, Paul.'

'It's a strong lead part and you'll have Willie as your co-star. You know how your fans love the two of you.'

Lilian was silent for a second or two. 'Paul, I think I may be in danger if I come back to Germany.'

'Nonsense. I'm working with Joseph Goebbels and told him about the film. He was very enthusiastic. You know of course he is the Minister of Propaganda; he has assured me that you are safe in Germany and would be the epitome of German womanhood in the film.'

Lilian pulled a face. 'Mm, well if you're sure. You know they've confiscated some of my property?'

'I'm sure it's only temporary. How about I arrange for half your money to be paid up front, how's that?'

'Well … when do you need me?'

'Can you make the first week in February?'

'Yes.'

'Good. Come over the weekend before, on Saturday, for dinner.'

'You're stark raving nuts!'

Lilian took the phone away from her ear and smiled; she re-arranged her hair and restored the receiver to the side of her head.

'And you know what will happen if that swine Otto gets hold of you.'

'Guy, it'll be okay. Don't worry. Anyway they won't do anything while I'm filming, so don't worry!'

'Well I guess I do worry. You know how fond I am of you.'

'I'm flattered. Especially when I know you have a girl in every port,' she added with a touch of sarcasm.

'Now that's not fair.'

'What about Kitty?'

'Ah, Kitty!'

'Yes, Kitty. One glance from you and she would drop everything, and I mean everything!'

'Now Lilian, you know we have a very good friendship at the moment, it's fun and nobody gets hurt.'

'True, although sometimes ...,' she paused and there was a moment's silence.

'Are you still there?'

'Yes. Do you know, Guy, sometimes you make me feel like a teenager. It's so frustrating.'

'Perhaps you need someone in your life.'

Lilian laughed. 'I have too many people. In the film world little fleas live on bigger fleas and big fleas live on even larger fleas and so on.'

'I didn't mean that.' Guy sighed.

'Darling, I'll call you in two weeks when I'm back in Berlin.'

'Of course. Just take care.' The phone clicked as Guy cut the line.

Lilian took the *Le Train Bleu* back from Cannes to Paris; she stayed with friends and whilst there met up with Jean Boyer, the French film director, who, on hearing of her present predicament in Germany, tried to get Lilian to play the lead in the latest film he was shooting in the summer. Leaving her options open, Lilian travelled on the express train, discreetly making her way back to her home in Berlin.

Chapter 16

Hitler had now been planning for some time to ignore the Munich Agreement and make a grab for the remainder of Czechoslovakia. Using his bully boy tactics, he forced the Czech president, Dr. Emil Hacha, to sign a surrender document or, as he put it, Hacha and his fellow countrymen would be violently crushed.

Chamberlain at last woke up to the fact that Hitler, with a catalogue of broken promises, had no intention of honouring the Munich Agreement. In the light of which, he went on to give his assurance to Poland that Britain would stand by her. This had the written support of France.

Enraged, Hitler knew he had finally found an opponent who would stand up and be counted. Even with a lukewarm reception from the German people and his closest ally, Italy, his country was closer to a war footing than ever before.

***

UFA, the film production company, was based in Babelsberg, Potsdam, about twenty kilometres south west of Berlin, whilst Lilian's house in Dahlem was half way between the two. Each morning the studio would send a car for Lilian and in the evening take her to wherever she wished to go.

For three weeks the shooting progressed steadily, although Lilian's working relationship with her ex-husband became distinctly fraught, particularly as the part was not to Lilian's liking, showing her in an unsympathetic light. In the last week of shooting, Paul lost his temper with Lilian on more than one occasion, leaving the actress in floods of tears. That night she telephoned Guy Parrett's office.

'Hello Guy. Thank God you are there.'

'You're lucky to catch me. Anyway I thought you were going to phone me when you got back.'

'I went up to Paris for a few days, stayed with some friends and then slipped back home.'

'No problems?'

Lilian hesitated. 'Well … '

'Come on, spit it out. What's wrong?'

'Well the film has just about finished, thank God. Paul has been horrid and when I complained about the script he said that Goebbels had read it and thought that it would be an ideal part for me.'

'And? … '

'Guy, it's bloody awful and now, because I complained, they've put a watch on me. A man has followed my car back home the last two nights. I think they plan to arrest me again.' There was silence on the telephone for several moments. Lilian raised her voice, 'Guy, are you still there?'

'Yes. Look I'm in the middle of an assignment. How many more days shooting have you got left?'

'Um … three at the most. We'll be finished this week. '

'Okay. I'll be at your house tomorrow when you get home. At what time?'

'Say six?'

'Fine. Just ignore anything or anybody and go

indoors and wait.'

'Thank you, Guy. I'm sorry I'm such a nuisance.'

'Rubbish, you're a victim of circumstances, that's all. Of course there is the fact that you couldn't wait for me to sweep you off your feet and whisper naughty things in your ear...'

'Guy! Thanks anyway!'

The next night, Lilian's chauffeured Mercedes approached the house and signalled to turn into the drive. As it slowed down, a man who appeared to be the gardener touched his old battered hat and moved his barrow out of the way. He continued sweeping the clippings from the large buddleia that had been overhanging the drive. When the car passed by, the man looked up and boldly winked at the actress. It was all Lilian could do to prevent herself from bursting out with laughter. The gardener was still sweeping a minute later when an Opel car pulled up. A man in a black full-length leather coat got out and approached the gardener.

'You!'

Slowly straightening up from his work, the man snatched off his hat and scratched his head. 'Sir.'

'Do you work here?'

'Sir.'

'Has your mistress come home?'

The gardener appeared to be hard of hearing and shuffled closer to the Gestapo officer. As he got nearer he put his hand to his ear. 'Pardon, sir.'

The man reeled back. 'Phew, you smell dreadful.' He turned on his heel and got back in the car.

It was at least a quarter of an hour later when Lilian heard a tap on the French windows and she let in a rather shabbily dressed Guy.

'What a brilliant disguise. But why were you so long? I've already finished my drink.'

'Hello Guy, how lovely to see you!' Guy replied in a falsetto voice. He leant across and kissed Lilian.

'Phew. Not only do you look dirty, but you smell as well.' Lilian screwed up her nose.

'Funny that's what the man said! Do you realise how long it took me to acquire this suave look?' he replied.

Standing back with her hands on her hips she regarded her visitor. 'Come to think about it, you would have made a great tramp.'

Guy walked across to the drinks cabinet. 'Mm ... too precarious. They get beaten up by the Gestapo.' He poured himself a drink.

Lilian came over and waved her empty glass at him.

'What are you drinking?' Guy took the glass.

'A Manhattan please, darling.'

As Guy mixed the drink, Lilian wandered over and draped herself over the sofa. 'I was right, wasn't I?'

'Oh yes. He was in an black Opel and not only that, he came back five minutes later. It was just as well I stayed because the car slowed down and, as if satisfied, he tapped the driver on the shoulder and it swiftly drove away. I should think he was going back to make his report.' Guy carried the drinks over to the sofa and sitting down, passed the cocktail to Lilian. He lifted his glass. 'Cheers'.

'Cheers. Thanks for coming.'

Guy grinned. 'That's okay, I told my editor I had a hot scoop.'

'Mm … you should be so lucky!'

'So what have you in mind?'

Lilian sipped her drink. 'I think I need to leave Germany.'

'Permanently?'

'I'm afraid it may have to be. This time I might

146

find it a bit more difficult. It was only Paul's influence with Goebbels that allowed me back. The Nazis are rather reticent about upsetting the world press, and all my fans.'

'Didn't you say that they had already confiscated some of your property?' Guy put his drink down and fished out a pack of cigarettes, offering one to Lilian.

She shook her head. 'They're too strong for me.' Giving the packet a brief glance, she nodded, 'Camels. How appropriate!' She reached out for the cigarette box, took out a cigarette and waited for Guy to give her a light.

Returning the pack to his pocket, Guy picked up his glass. 'You didn't answer my question.'

'They have appropriated my Baden Baden property, they say they need it for training purposes. It isn't far from the French border but I rarely use it. Paul persuaded me to buy it and told me it would be a good investment.'

'How about readies?'

Lilian gave Guy a puzzled look. 'What?'

'You know - dollars, greenbacks, marks, whatever - ready cash.'

'Oh, well they've just paid me several thousand

marks for this film. It's supposed to be fifty per cent up front as a sweetener.'

'Okay. What happens if they find out that you've left Germany?'

Lilian shrugged. 'I suppose they may try to get it all back, as well as grabbing anything else I leave behind.'

Guy got up and paced across the room. 'Just suppose we use the same ruse this Friday and as soon as you've finished, we drive down to Antibes?'

Lilian shook her head. 'They would spot it straight away. Especially if we drove south instead of returning to Berlin.'

Guy continued his pacing.

'Of course,' began Lilian thoughtfully, 'if we went to Magdeburg which is about twenty kilometres south west, we could visit my father's grave'

'What then?'

'We switch cars and go south!'

Guy nodded. 'Even better if we could get them to follow your official car back to Dahlem.'

'One other thing. If I give you a banker's draft for, say, seventy-five thousand Reichmarks. could you pay it into your bank?'

Guy stopped in his tracks and stared at Lilian. 'Gee, … that's about thirty thousand dollars. Firstly my banker will have a heart attack and secondly, do you trust me?' He grinned.

'Of course I trust you. And as far as my bank goes, they are quite used to me spending large sums! Oh, and one other thing, not Antibes. I've had a tentative offer of a film in France, Paris to be exact.'

Friday dawned and Lilian's limousine arrived early. As the car left the drive, Lilian, seated in the back, totally ignored the Gestapo officer who was waiting outside in his black Opel.

There was no actual filming taking place on the Friday, but the publicity people were taking camera shots and finalising the press releases.

Lilian took Paul to one side and nervously explained that she wished to leave early and visit her father's grave in Magdeburg. To her relief he agreed. Having thanked him, she said goodbye to the cast, giving out little presents to all involved, including the crew.

Her car arrived and it was a relieved Lilian who waved goodbye as she set off for Magdeburg. In less than half an hour she stepped out of the limousine and walked into the cemetery. There was a cold wind blowing and Lilian pulled up the collar of her coat, and looked back to the road where a black Opel was pulling up. Nervously she carried a large bunch of flowers and laid it down on the side of the grave. She picked up an empty vase and walked across to the small building nearby to fill it with water.

A few minutes later she emerged carefully carrying the vase full of water to the graveside. It took a few minutes to arrange the flowers and when she had finished, lowered her head for a moment before turning and walking back to the car.

The man in the Opel threw away his cigarette, started his engine and followed the limousine back east.

Chapter 17

Guy lowered his newspaper and watched an old lady slowly leave the cemetery and walk across to his car. She opened the front passenger door and got in beside him.

'A great performance, doll!'

The old lady leant across and kissed him. 'What do you expect? I must say you smell a bit better than last time we met!'

Guy ignored her jibe. 'How was Kitty?'

'Very cold and very grumpy,' Lilian divested herself of a grey wig and her clothes, throwing them onto the back seat of the Volkswagen.

'What will she do?'

'I've arranged for her to stay the night at my house and then leave early tomorrow morning when she will catch a train to Paris.'

'Where will you stay?'

'I've rented a small apartment on the Boulevard Saint Germain. I'm afraid it's too small for you to stay, especially as Kitty will be there as well.'

Guy started the engine and slowly moved out into

the traffic. 'Don't worry I have newspaper contacts in Paris.'

Lilian gave a rare smile. 'Kitty will be jealous.'

It was a heady time for Lilian in Paris. Thanks to her new director, Jean Boyer, she had been introduced into the French film society. At present her finances were liquid and while they lasted she enjoyed a whirl of glamour. It helped to be where the French courtiers still supported the film world, advertising their wares.

Her first French film was appropriate, in that it portrayed Franz Schubert and his amorous adventures with an English dancer. Entitled *Serenade,* it was completed before the end of August 1939, which was when Guy, who had gone back to Germany the previous month, decided to return to Paris.

The door bell rang, interrupting Lilian's telephone conversation with her director. Excusing herself, she replaced the receiver and went to the door.

'Hi!' Guy Parrett stood there with a large grin and a huge bunch of roses.

'Well don't just stand there, you'd better come in!' Lilian held the door of her flat open for Guy, then turned back to let him follow her down a long corridor.

'Well I guess you found a great apartment.'

'It's small and compact, ideal for my purpose,' Lilian answered over her shoulder as she led him into a huge sitting room with large windows overlooking the Boulevard Saint Germain.

'Phew, if this is a small apartment, I'll eat my hat!' replied Guy as he presented Lilian with the bouquet.

'Thank you, Guy, they're beautiful. Help yourself to a drink and pour me one whilst I find a vase.'

'Say, it's a bit early for me.'

'Nonsense!' came the reply from another room.

'Oh well, what the hell.' He walked across to a well stocked drinks trolley and poured out two drinks.

After five minutes, Lilian reappeared bearing a large floral arrangement. 'Now then, what's the news from Berlin?'

Guy grimaced. 'Sorry to disappoint you. I've been pulled out by my chief and he has relocated our office here in Paris. We've still got a contact or two but it was getting more and more difficult for me to move around. Your friend Goebbels has made life hell and so has your bête noir, Otto Heinrich. He would just love to

153

get his hands on me.'

Guy took the drinks over to Lilian who had collapsed into a deep armchair. He sat down opposite her and raised his glass.

'To absent friends - which reminds me, where is Kitty?'

'She'll be in soon.' Lilian got up and walked over to the fireplace. 'Have you found anywhere to stay?' she asked, changing the subject.

'Oh yes, a fellow journalist has let me share.'

'Good.' Lilian picked up a silver cigarette box and offered it to Guy. He shook his head and watched as she selected one and lit it from a matching silver lighter.

Guy began to feel there was something wrong. 'By the way, I've still got your money. I put it in my account here in Paris so it should be easy to transfer.'

Lilian stopped pacing and turned to face Guy. 'Oh Guy, I'm sorry. To tell the truth, I've been worried sick. The Gestapo have seized all my assets and frozen my German bank accounts. I'm having to rely on my latest film here in France for funds but luckily, they have another film for me. Of course I've my villa down south but I must have some income.' She sat down next to Guy.

'Well, now you have some funds, so that's settled. How about we go out to dinner tonight?'

Lilian clapped her hands. 'Oh, that's a wonderful idea and we can go on to a great jazz club I've discovered here in Saint Germain. They've lots of visiting artists playing jazz quite informally. '

They were interrupted by Kitty's arrival and this time Lilian insisted on opening a bottle of champagne to celebrate. After a while Guy made a discreet exit having arranged to visit the bank that afternoon to transfer Lilian's funds.

The entrance to Le Jazz Hot was down some steps to a small courtyard where a man stood smoking a cigarette by a dimly lit door; from the doorway came the high-pitched wail of a clarinet.

The three made their way into the cellar which had a haze of Gauloise smoke floating in the dim lighting. They were shown to a small table squeezed in between several others. A girl arrived with a carafe of red wine and three glasses, exchanging them for a banknote produced by Guy. He thanked her with a wave of his hand as the noise from the band was such that talking was virtually impossible.

For about a quarter of an hour the members of the band played a variety of jazz and at one point they were joined by a dark haired, slightly swarthy guitarist who was obviously a favourite with the audience.

Lilian tapped Guy's sleeve and pointed to the new guitarist. Leaning forward she shouted in Guy's ear, 'Django Reinhardt.' She gestured with her thumb and forefinger, a sign of approval.

After a while the musicians took a break and the three were able to talk amongst themselves. Guy glanced at some of the clientele. They were a mixture of age and, by their appearance, of affluence.

A black man got up from a nearby table and, obviously egged on by his friends, strode over to the piano. Sitting down he began to play various easy numbers. Guy glanced over as he started to play an American composition.

'Well I'll be ... The last time I saw that guy, he was playing in a club in New York.'

Kitty looked over her shoulder at the man. 'Oh you mean Sam? He's often in here, usually with that rather dishy American; someone told me he was a gun runner or something. Um ... Blaine ... Richard Blaine.'

Guy looked back at the table, where the

156

American, who happened to be facing him, nodded. Kitty turned to Guy, 'Do you know him?'

Guy nodded. 'Yeah, Rick. He left New York in rather a hurry. It was rumoured he had an affair and the husband shot the wife and tried to blame Blaine.'

'The girl with him is very pretty,' Kitty added.

'Oh, Rick could pick 'em okay.'

Eventually the pianist got up from the piano and his party rose to leave. As they went past, the American leant over and whispered something to Guy. At that moment the band returned and settled down to play hot jazz. After one particularly noisy number, Guy suggested they should leave. Nodding, the two girls got up and led the way out. Once they were on the street, Lilian turned to Guy.

'What was that all about? What did the man whisper to you?'

Guy looked back at the entrance to the club. 'Apparently the two men at the corner table were Gestapo spies. And they were taking an inordinate amount of interest in us!'

Chapter 18

On August 25th 1939, Britain and Poland signed a Mutual Assistance Treaty; this was more than fortuitous as just one week later Germany invaded Poland.

Two days later, on September 3rd, Britain, France, Australia and New Zealand declared war on Germany.

Thus began what was known as the phoney war, which lasted until May 10th 1940, when the Germans invaded France. During that time there was no real land offensive by the Allies.

***

It was a bit of luck for Lilian that her new film was not only wrapped up but released ten days before the German invasion, and by then Lilian and Kitty had left Paris and were living in her villa in Antibes.

It was here, early one morning, when Lilian was

sitting with a cup of coffee and listening to the wireless, that she heard the news of Dunkirk.

Shocked, she called out for Kitty. 'Kitty! Come quickly, it's terrible news. They're evacuating the expeditionary forces from Dunkirk's beaches.'

A few minutes later, Kitty appeared with a towel wrapped around her. 'What does it mean?'

'We've lost. The Nazis are everywhere and the French army has been beaten.'

Kitty automatically tightened the towel around her. 'Are we in danger here?'

'I don't know!'

'What should we do?'

'I suppose it depends on how long we can defend this part of France.' Lilian got up and turned the wireless off. 'We need some information. Do you think Guy is still in Paris?'

'I doubt it. Don't forget they said the Gestapo had a black list and as soon as they got to Paris, they would round up those people on their list. Guy was certainly on their list, even if he was American and they aren't that far away from the capital.' She sat down at the table and poured herself some coffee.

'Perhaps we should go back to America?' Lilian

mused.

'Well that wasn't a howling success last time,' replied Kitty.

'I know, but we would be safe and I'm sure the studio would find me something to do. Even if they don't, we have enough friends over there and I suppose we should do something to help the war effort.'

'Lilian, you're half German. Do you think they would believe you?'

Lilian scowled at her companion. 'I certainly do *not* support those murdering Nazis. Of course they'll believe me!'

They listened to the news on and off all morning, but it didn't stop Kitty from taking a swim in the pool. Some neighbours Lilian had met in Paris, came to lunch. The discussion was mainly about the war and what they would all do if the Germans arrived in the south of France. Except for the fact that they would have to leave, no one could think of a safer haven than the United States of America, but the question was when should they leave.

They were just finishing lunch when a car came up the drive. The iron pergola with its covering of bougainvillea and magenta flowers hid the car from view.   Seconds later, the grim face of Guy appeared round the corner of the villa.   He walked along the terrace, under a purple covering of wisteria, to where the party were sitting and kissed Lilian and Kitty before introductions were made to their guests.   Pulling out a chair he sat down heavily, sighing deeply.

Lilian stood up. 'Guy, you look tired.   Would you like a drink before I get you something to eat?'

Guy nodded with a weak smile.   'The news is grim. They're evacuating large numbers from Dunkirk but how many they will save is anyone's guess.'

'We heard the news, but they are a little cagey. What's the latest?'

He accepted the glass from Lilian and sipped the wine before answering.   'They are saying the Germans will be in Paris within a fortnight.   If they are, it'll all be over.   The word is that the Government will capitulate rather than allow the people to be massacred.'

'So what do we do?'

'I think you should leave.   I'll drive over to Nice Airport this afternoon and see what outbound flights there are.   I've a contact there, but the phone lines are jammed.   Tomorrow I'll drive to Marseille and see what the shipping situation is.'

'Guy, have you eaten today?' Kitty interrupted. When he shook his head, she got up and went into the villa.

Lilian's neighbours took the opportunity to thank her for their lunch and as she walked down the drive with them, they promised to keep an eye on the villa if she decided to leave France.

Kitty reappeared with a tray of goodies for Guy. 'Here you are. I can recommend the ham. Can I get you anything else?'

On impulse he took her hand and gently pulled her towards him. The kiss was unexpected and for a second or two she froze before responding enthusiastically. 'Oh, Guy! I think you'd do anything for food.'

'Of course!'

Embarrassed, Kitty set about clearing the table as Lilian walked back across the terrace.

'Oh good, Kitty is looking after you.' Lilian glanced at her friend and smiled as she observed her flushed face. Later that afternoon she made no comment when Guy drove Kitty down to the town centre before driving on to Nice.

It was past seven in the evening before he returned. Lilian and Kitty were back on the terrrace having drinks. As Guy walked across to them he couldn't help thinking how ironic the setting must have looked to an outsider. The scene was so peaceful, even idyllic.

Lilian stood up and poured out a cocktail for Guy. 'This should remind you of better times.'

Guy gratefully accepted the drink and sank into a comfortable wicker chair. 'Oh, you have no idea how much I needed that. The airport was utter chaos. It took me over an hour to reach my contact and then it was a waste of time. All flights are either cancelled or booked for at least a fortnight ahead. The military have taken over the airport and the Air Force are using it as a base. We'll have to find another route.'

'Will you go to Marseille tomorrow?' Kitty asked.

'Well I think it would be best if I contacted the American consul first. I could try the British consul but they would only let you in, Lilian. Kitty has a Swedish passport.'

'Could we get into the States?' Lilian asked.

'Probably. It's our best bet,' Guy replied.

The next few days were incredibly frustrating for

the friends, the more so as the information coming through American and British consulates and embassies was virtually useless, although through no fault of their own. It did seem that it might be better to make for Algiers or Gibraltar. Spain was still recovering from its Civil War and the roads to Portugal were in a bad way. It was all building up to a nasty climax.

Chapter 19

By mid May 1940, the Germans had driven the Allies, including the B.E.F., back to the coast. By 20th May, Lord Gort had started planning Operation Dynamo, the evacuation of the troops from Dunkirk.

The French First Army with just 40,000 men defended Lille, standing in the way of seven German divisions including two armoured brigades; they were to fight a heroic rearguard action.

The B.E.F. had been ordered back to Dunkirk where on the 26th May, the first of 600 ships took off 7,669 allied soldiers. By the end of the eighth day this had risen to 338,226.

There was no stopping the Germans and ten days later they marched into Paris. The French Government eventually surrendered on the 22nd of June, 1940.

The Germans, recognising the enormity of the task in controlling the whole of France, agreed with the French Government in Vichy, to divide the country in two. Whilst the north would be under German administration and rule, the south would be administered by the French, from Vichy, but still ruled by Germany.

***

'Guy, I'm sure that it'll be alright if I stay here.' Lilian carried on deadheading roses in one of the borders.

Guy, who was trying to have a conversation with the elusive actress, trailed around after her, reluctantly carrying a trug of freshly cut blooms. 'I think it'll be fine until the Germans get your local police to round up any people on their black lists. At present they're too busy with Paris and the northern cities, although there could come a time, God only knows, when the allies will return and it doesn't take much to realise that France has a soft underbelly.'

'Well until I have to leave, I'm staying put!'

'Okay, but I must contact our London office. We

have a man in Nice. I'll go down to see him later this week.'

'I appreciate you have to go,' Lilian continued, 'why don't you take Kitty with you?'

'To Nice?'

'No. To the States.'

'What about you?'

Lilian sighed. 'Oh come on, Guy. I shall be fine and my last trip to the States was a disaster.'

'You're being very defeatist and, if I may say so, stupid.'

Lilian glanced with surprise at Guy. 'Charming! Anyway, I love it here and that's that. Now I'm off down the village to pick up a few things. What are you going to do?'

'After making a few phone calls I thought I'd go down to the beach for a swim.'

'You'd better take Kitty with you, she's frightened and I think a little put out that you tend to ignore her.'

'Oh nuts! She knows I'm very fond of her.'

'Fond wasn't the word she was hoping for.'

'Do you think - lusting after - might have been more to her taste?'

'Well I wouldn't put it so crudely.'

'I suppose it's because of you and me ...' Guy began.

Lilian turned on him with a stern face. 'Guy, you know that's not true. There's never been anything between us that would make her think otherwise.'

For a few seconds there was silence as Lilian turned and examined the rose bush she had been pruning.

'What about your first trip to the States on board the liner, especially after that fracas with the German agent?'

Lilian turned back to Guy with a mischievous grin. 'What about it?'

'Enough to know that it took you a lot of talking, to your husband and the press, to convince them we were just good friends!'

'We are!'

'Mmm...' Guy grinned. 'I think I'll make my calls before finding Kitty and offering a quick seduction job on the beach.'

Guy was quite surprised to see Lilian driving back up to the house before he had finished his calls. She made her way across the terrace where Kitty was reading a book and Guy was sitting writing notes.

'Hello, I thought you were going shopping, that was quick?' Guy looked up from writing.

Lilian grimaced. 'I was, but I had a bit of a shock. You know Leon, the café owner?'

Guy nodded.

'While he was serving me coffee he discreetly informed me that the local gendarmerie had been given a list of people wanted by the Gestapo ...' Lilian paused.

'And?'

'My name was on it!'

'Oh, my God!' Kitty put her hand to her mouth.

'That was quick.' Guy put down his pen.

'Well it appeared the local gendarmes are not happy about informing on their neighbours. Even so, there are always collaborators in every town and Leon suggested I should start thinking about leaving.'

'Well, are you thinking about it?' said Guy.

I suppose so. We could wait and see what happens in Paris.'

'Lilian. You have to go *now*.' Kitty said forcefully.

'She's right. You have no option,' Guy added, before getting up and pouring out drinks. 'There's a boat for the States leaving Lisbon in ten days, I think I can get berths. It won't be luxury, but it will get us away.'

Lilian sighed. 'Of course, you're right. Well let's have lunch and then we can make plans this afternoon.'

After two days everything was settled and Lilian had arranged to let the house to a French family she had known in Paris. She and Kitty managed to raise sufficient cash from their local friends without too much trouble. Guy completed all the formalities and they were ready to leave in two days' time. It would take at least three days to motor to Lisbon, providing they had no problems at the border.

It was seven o'clock on the morning of their departure as they were sitting having breakfast, served by a tearful maid, when the front doorbell jangled.

'Who on earth is that at this God-awful hour?' exclaimed Guy.

'Probably some neighbour, wishing us luck,' Lilian replied as she reached for a croissant.

'I'll go,' Kitty jumped up enthusiastically, 'we have some lovely neighbours who've helped us out. It would be churlish to ignore them.'

They were still surmising which of their

neighbours it was, when Kitty came back ashen-faced. Two seconds later she was followed in by a file of men, led by Otto Heinrich.

Chapter 20

Otto stood triumphantly over Lilian, as one of his henchman held a pistol to Guy's head. The maid, who had been cooking some bacon at the stove, was now weeping uncontrollably, cowering in the corner of the kitchen.

'You've no jurisdiction in this part of France,' protested Guy.

'Technically you're all subject to the rule of the Third Reich. You're all wanted in connection with helping Jews to escape from Germany,' Otto retorted.

'The government in Vichy ...' began Guy.

'The government in Vichy is under the control of our beloved leader. We are here to enforce his laws.' Otto waved to two of his men. 'Now take these three upstairs and get them to pack for the journey. ' He turned back. 'You're all going back to Germany, you may have one suitcase of clothes, nothing else. You!' He pointed at the maid, 'I'll have that bacon which is beginning to burn and some coffee. After that you'll get something to eat for my men.' He went to put his arm around Lilian, 'You're lucky I'm just hungry. Now go!'

The men herded the three towards the kitchen door.   Lilian stopped.   'My friend is Swedish   and Mr. Parrett is American.   They're not at war with Germany, so you must let them go.'

'Miss Harvey!' Otto sneered, 'you're in no position to   make demands.   Just watch your step or I'll let my men find ways of making you and your Swedish friend comply with my wishes.'

Guy lunged towards Otto only to be pistol whipped, which forced him to stagger towards the kitchen door.   He grabbed the handle for support.   Kitty attempted to help him but she too was manhandled by one of their captors.

Otto laughed cruelly.   'Resistance is useless, my friends.' He was still laughing as he took a seat at the breakfast table.

One of Lilian's neighbours had started to walk up the drive that morning, carrying a small parcel as a parting gift.   He stopped when a stumbling figure ran towards him.   Recognising Natalie, the girl who looked after the house for Lilian, who also came from his home village just outside Cannes, he realised when she got closer that she was sobbing.

'Why Natalie, whatever is the matter?'

She cried. 'Monsieur. It is the Germans! They've arrested Madame and her friends.'

'Mon Dieu. Are they there now?'

'Yes they're eating breakfast, then they intend to drive them back to Germany,' she sobbed again. 'They've got guns and threatened us but I managed to escape out of the back door.'

'Quick, come with me, they must not see you leave. How do you know they're going to take them back to Germany?' he asked, taking her arm and hurrying her back down the drive.

'They were arguing about which way to drive. I think they're nervous about being seen. They're all in civilian clothes, but I'm sure they are the Gestapo.'

'So which way are they travelling?'

'That's just it. They decided on the route to Grasse, which goes through my village.'

The man led Natalie down a gravel path towards his cottage. 'Good, it'll take them at least half an hour to pass through the village. Let us hear what Pierre has to say.'

The Germans bundled Lilian into the lead car, which also

carried Otto and two of his men. Guy and Kitty were forced into the second car with the remaining four men. Reluctantly Otto had given orders for the house and its contents not to be touched. He was not absolutely certain that his actions would be approved of by his superiors, but his obsession with Lilian, particularly with the assistance she'd given to Jens, had come to a head. This was his revenge. He could hardly wait to get back to Germany.

The large limousines swept out of the drive and were soon into the outskirts of Cannes.

Otto took out a silver cigarette case and offered it to Lilian. 'It's a ten hour drive, I think it would be a good idea to relax. After all, once you are back in Germany your comforts may be few.' Lilian gave him a cold shoulder, staring out of the window at the suburbs of Cannes. She knew that once in Germany she would be at Otto's mercy. If she didn't give in to him he would take great delight in passing her around his favoured henchmen.

Putting a cigarette into a holder, he lit up. 'Of course we could come to some understanding.' He smiled and laid his hand on Lilian's thigh. His smile turned to a scowl as she lifted his sleeve with two fingers and disdainfully dropped his hand back in his own lap. It was sheer bravado. Inside her stomach was in knots.

The cars took the road inland towards Grasse and after half an hour entered the village of Saint Vallier de Thiey. Lilian recognised the name as the home of her maid, Natalie. She wondered what had happened to her. Somehow she had disappeared and from the sound of the raised voices of the Gestapo - for that's what they were - she had escaped into the back garden.

By now it was late morning and, except for a few goats, the road was empty. Houses became fewer and several kilometres out of the village the road began to wind through an extremely rocky terrain.

Rounding a particularly tight corner, the driver of the lead car had to slam on his brakes. A gendarme was holding up his hand to stop them. The following car swerved to avoid him and ran into some rocks on the verge, puncturing the tyre on the nearside front wheel. Otto said something to the man in the front passenger seat and they got out of the car. He shouted at the gendarme, who shrugged his shoulders and pointed at his car which appeared to have driven into the back of a hay-cart which now blocked the road. Swearing, Otto walked back to the second car. His men had got out and were standing round discussing the damaged wheel.

Turning red with rage he cuffed the driver. 'Dolt! You fool, I had planned for us to have lunch in Grasse. You've lost your chance of any lunch. You!' he pointed to one of the other men, 'help this fool change the tyre. The rest of you come and help that idiot of a gendarme to move his car and the cart. We're wasting time.'

Lilian looked through the back window at the car behind them, wondering if Guy would attempt anything. But Otto had taking the precaution of locking the car they were in. It would be pointless trying to move it, particularly as one of the men had jammed rocks under the wheels to stop it slipping when they jacked it up.

Otto was still shouting, this time at the poor farmer who was trying to calm the donkey in the front of the cart.

As Lilian watched, Otto raised his pistol and held it to the man's head. Mercifully he didn't pull the trigger, but laughed at the man cowering pitifully.

It was after he holstered his gun and turned to his men, who had their shoulders to the gendarme's vehicle, that Lilian saw two men appear behind him. Carrying rifles they crept up behind Otto and one jabbed his gun into the back of Otto's neck.

The two were suddenly joined by several others who surrounded the men at the second car. The leader of what appeared to be a group of partisans, who had the gun to the back of Otto's neck, waved the Germans to the side of the road and then peered into the lead car. Seeing Lilian he opened the door and helped her out.

'Miss Harvey, are you okay? Is there anything you need before I take these scum and shoot them.'

Recovering her composure, Lilian glanced towards the second car. 'My friends. I have two friends with me. This man has locked them in that car.'

'That's no problem.' He shouted instructions and one of his men discovered the keys, which had quickly appeared in the trembling hand of the driver. Released, Guy and Kitty struggled out of the car, where their hands were untied.

'Thank God for the cavalry!' drawled Guy, rubbing his wrists, 'what do we do now?'

The leader of the partisans chuckled. 'I think you should get the hell out of here. We'll dispose of the two German cars before we shoot the bastards.'

Guy looked at him in surprise. 'Are you American?'

'Yup. Sure am. It's a long story and we don't have time, so as the French say, 'au revoir', buddy.'

'No wait!' Guy pointed to the Germans who were being led up the hillside. 'Look, I don't think they were supposed to be here. That man ...', he pointed to Otto, 'is a fanatic. Determined to arrest Miss Lilian Harvey, I don't think he will report his failure. Can you keep him, for say three days, to allow us to get out of France?'

'Sure. No problem, buddy.'

Guy held out his hand. 'The name's Guy. Who am I thanking?'

'Buddy!'

Kitty laughed. 'All you Americans are mad.'

'Mad we may be, miss, but sure useful when the time comes. Now if you check carefully you'll find that the cop car isn't damaged. When we're out of sight the cop will drive you back, but I warn you, get out of France while you can.'

He turned and strode over to where his men were waiting at the bottom of the track up the hillside. They stood for a few moments and watched him go.

'Madame,' the gendarme stood behind them. He looked at Lilian and smiled. 'I'm Pierre, Natalie's brother. She warned us you were coming this way. Luckily a friend contacted me and, let us just say, not all the French people are behind this Vichy government. Now if you, monsieur, would just help my father and me get all this hay off my car, we'll be on our way.'

Chapter21

The Vichy government were in a huge dilemma over their navy, who had played a part in the evacuation at Dunkirk.

The Admiral of the French fleet, François Darlan, told Churchill that the fleet would be sunk before it surrendered to the Germans.

Churchill was very aware that Hitler would dearly like to appropriate the ships, preferably manning them with German sailors to fight against the Allies.

In the light of this, Churchill gave the French an ultimatum to sail their fleets to an Allied port or they would be sunk; however he found it difficult to persuade the British government that this was the best course of action.

Ultimately Darlan ordered the French fleet, off Oran on the African coast, to sail to a port in the USA. Almost immediately the

British intercepted an order by the Vichy government to send reinforcements to Oran.

Churchill decided not to pussy-foot around any more and attacked. Some ships escaped, but it was the end to Hitler's dream of acquiring the French fleet. Churchill had made his point to the world, that he would never make peace with Hitler and would fight to the finish.

Thus the various French fleets were warned as the British blockaded them and at Toulon, in particular, staying in port until late in 1942 when the Germans invaded the 'South Zone' and the French scuttled their ships.

Prior to this time it did not stop the occasional small craft sailing on exercise along the south coast.

***

After arriving back at the villa the three friends continued their original plans to leave the following morning.

Natalie was delighted to see them and promised to look after the villa whilst Lilian was away, until the friends from Paris arrived.

Guy spent most of the afternoon on the phone, eventually catching up with the girls at about six o'clock. Walking out onto the terrace he found the two of them sipping cocktails as though they hadn't a care in the world. 'Great. I've been working my butt off and you two drown your sorrows. Although it doesn't look like sorrows to me!'

'I'll have you know, we've packed everything,' Lilian pouted.

'Well I guess you had better unpack. The border's tighter than a duck's arse. We'll have to think of another way. I might do it on my own, but not with you two. Italy's out, as is the Spanish border. And I don't fancy climbing the Pyrenees.

'What about a boat?'

'Too far, unless we can commandeer a destroyer.'

'A friend of mine has a yacht … ,' Lilian stopped as Guy snapped his fingers.

'Destroyer! '

'You think we can find a destroyer?' replied Kitty sarcastically.

'I don't know, but the French fleet is bottled up in Toulon. My contacts tell me the Vichy government refuse to hand it over to the Brits who have their fleet off the coast. I do know there was an American destroyer on standby to extricate any Americans who got caught up in the Spanish conflict and stayed on. I heard a rumour that they were seen off the French coast. If only I could get word to them.' Guy picked up Kitty's glass and drained it before going back into the house, smiling at Kitty's half-hearted protest.

About half an hour later Guy borrowed Lilian's car and drove over to Nice. He hadn't returned that night when Lilian and Kitty went to bed.

At breakfast the next morning they were very subdued. Kitty looked nervously across the table. 'Do you think Guy's alright? I mean, he could have been arrested or even had an accident.'

Lilian shook her head. 'Not Guy, he's tough. Obstinate, but tough. He'll try every angle. I think it's the journalist streak in him.'

The morning dragged on as the women made themselves useful around the house, doing odd jobs. It wasn't until nearly midday they heard a car coming up the drive. Excitedly they both rushed out to greet Guy, who wearily climbed out of the car.

Kitty threw her arms around him. 'Oh Guy, we thought we'd lost you!'

Extricating himself from Kitty's embrace, Guy took her hand and led them towards the house. 'Let's go inside, we've a lot to plan and I need a cup of coffee.'

Lilian made some more coffee and then sat down opposite Guy. 'Well?'

'Okay, it's fixed. The Americans do have a destroyer. They've had a presence here in the Med ever since they helped to evacuate their nationals from the Spanish Civil War. It can be ten miles off the coast at dawn in two days' time.'

'How on earth did you convince them that Kitty and I were Americans?'

'I didn't have to. The Captain was a fan of yours and when I said you were going over to play to the troops, he was all too keen to help,' Guy chuckled.

'Do you know, I think I will offer my services for war work. I really have lost my enthusiasm for films. Unless I get offered something sensational,' sighed Lilian.

'Well let's get there first!' Guy said. 'There's just one problem. We have to find a boat to take us out to the destroyer.'

'Guy, we have great faith in you.' said Kitty.

'Maybe, but I'm not sure where to start looking.'

'Mm … ' Lilian got up from the table. 'Kitty can you prepare lunch? I'm going down to the village. I should be back before two. Amuse yourselves, which shouldn't be too difficult.' She gave them a broad smile and taking up her bag she left them staring at her retreating figure.

It was well gone two by the time Lilian returned. She strode across the terrace to where Guy and Kitty were sipping drinks under the shade of the pergola.

'I hope you saved me some lunch.'

'Of course. We waited for you. Now sit down and tell us what this is all about.' Guy pulled out a chair for Lilian, then after pouring out a drink for her sat back expectantly.

Lilian smiled smugly. 'As Guy would say, it's all about contacts. 'I've found a boat!'

'How? When?' Guy leant forward and smacked his fist into his other hand. 'Where did you find this miracle?'

'Right under our noses. You remember I told you

about Leon at the café tipping me off about the Vichy directive? Well I guessed he was the most likely to help especially as he knows all the local fisherman. '

'And?'

'He gave me a coffee and within minutes he was back with an answer. A boat will be available at dawn the day after tomorrow. We must be at his café by four in the morning.'

Kitty clapped her hands, 'Lilian you're wonderful!'

'I have to agree with Kitty.' Guy nodded. 'I was more than a little worried as to how we would get out to the destroyer. May I ask how much our passage will cost?'

'No! It's all settled. Now let's have that lunch. I'm starving.'

Leon's bar was closed and barred, but there was a side entrance and when Guy tried the door it swung silently open. Inside the back room a little huddle of people stood nervously, each clutching the one suitcase they were allowed to take. Lilian smiled and embraced the proprietor.

'Bien. Venez, après moi.' He led the way through a back door and down some stone steps to a cellar. It was badly lit and the stairs were uneven. One of the women slipped and fell against the damp wall with a sob. Leon turned and put a finger to his lips.

There was a passage off the cellar which ran for about twenty yards, at the end of which was a bolted door. The café owner eased back the bolts which were well greased and made little noise. When he opened the door wind blew the warm rain into their faces.

Lilian grimaced as she followed the others out onto a wet stone jetty below the quay; in front of them was a small fishing trawler, its funnel sending out wisps of grey smoke.

Once aboard, the party were seated in a small cabin that stank of fish.

'When you next book tickets, Lilian, do choose something a little less aromatic!' murmured Kitty.

'Just you wait until we're out at sea. You may have something to complain about,' replied Guy.

Any further conversation was impossible because the deep throb of the engines cut in and revved up. The crew cast off and within a couple of minutes they were under way.

Apart from once when the cabin door opened and the captain looked in and nodded, the passengers sat on the wooden benches and stared apprehensively at the rain which beat at the windows.

After they had been going about thirty minutes, the captain put his head around the door and beckoned for Guy to follow him. They made their way up on to the tiny bridge where the captain pointed back at the shore. Coming out of the murky visibility was a high speed launch, less than a mile away.

'What is it?' Guy asked.

The captain studied the boat through his binoculars. 'Not good. It's a Vichy patrol boat.'

'How much further until we reach the destroyer?'

'Too far, probably about forty minutes. That launch will reach us in less than ten minutes. It could cause a real problem, but we'll just have to try and bluff it out. You had better go down and warn them to lie low. They might try and shoot it out. The only consolation is they will probably only have a machine gun!'

'Only!' Guy gave a sarcastic laugh and went below.

Chapter 22

For several minutes the escapees sat in the cabin listening to the throb of the engines. Quite soon they heard the higher pitch of the motor boat coming alongside and the sound of a loudhailer. Guy waved all the occupants onto the cabin floor and then, donning a waterproof, he went out on deck. It wasn't a patrol boat, but a high speed launch flying the Vichy flag. It had three men on board, one of whom had the loudhailer and was ordering them, in the name of the Vichy government, to give way.

The captain throttled back until they were just making headway. 'What is it you want?' he shouted.

'Have you any passengers?'

'Only my crew. We are on a fishing trip.'

'We wish to board you. Stop your engines.'

'What for? On whose authority are you acting? For all I know you might be pirates!' retorted the captain.

'If you don't do as we ask it will be worse for you.' The man lifted a pistol and fired a shot across the top of the wheelhouse. The captain automatically ducked, then taking the wheel from his helmsman, he swung the boat towards the launch which veered away, but not before another shot hit the man who had been at the wheel. He slumped to the floor clutching his arm. Keeping low, Guy managed to get to him. It was only a flesh wound but it was bleeding profusely.

'We'll try and keep them at bay, but they'll hit and run. The cabin walls won't stop a bullet, so tell all the passengers to lie flat on the floor,' the captain shouted as he swung the wheel. There was a whine from the launch coming in fast and turning away, but not before a fusillade of shots hit the boat. This time there was a scream from inside. Guy ran across the deck and entered the cabin. One of the other travellers was slumped on the floor.

'He stood up, trying to see what was going on,' said Lilian. She and Kitty were trying to staunch the blood from a shoulder wound.

'Keep him low and stay down yourselves,' ordered Guy as he left the cabin.

The launch had swung away in a half circle and was now following them. Guy went back to the wheelhouse.

'They've got a machine pistol,' announced the captain grimly, 'have you got any arms?'

Guy shook his head. 'What do you think they'll do next?'

'Hit and run. We're built like a tank and they are no match for us if we could ram them. But they could stop us with a lucky shot or two.'

Guy thought for a moment and then said 'Have you any flares?'

'Distress flares?'

'Yes. We could put them off for a bit longer. And with a bit of luck we might do some damage.'

'Unlikely, but they're in that locker and the cartridges are in a box.'

Guy found the pistol and loaded it just before the captain shouted a word of warning. The launch screamed past and then throttled right back to come level and one of the men emptied a magazine into the boat. When the firing stopped Guy peered round the wheelhouse door and swore. The third man on board the launch was none other than Otto Heinrich. Seeing the American, Otto raised his pistol and fired blindly at the trawler.

As the launch swung away once again Guy aimed the flare pistol and squeezed the trigger. The flare hit the screen of the launch and careered into space. Startled, the man at the wheel pulled it hard round and the boat moved out of range. Meantime the flare cracked open about one hundred yards further out into the Mediterranean. It might have been raining and the visibility poor but the red glare at around fifty feet above the sea was startling and lasted several minutes.

'Well that gave them something to think about,' Guy grinned as he went back into the wheelhouse. 'The man who last shot at us is a Gestapo officer, who's obsessed with capturing Miss Harvey. He'll stop at nothing.'

'If they empty another magazine into us like the last one he's sure to do some damage, probably kill one of us if not all.'

'How far have we got to go?'

'Still too far, probably three or four miles. It's difficult to see in this drizzle. '

Guy looked back at the boat which was just visible about one hundred yards behind them. 'There is that one option. We could try ramming them.'

The captain shook his head, 'I doubt if we would be quick enough. It doesn't look good.' The sound of the launch rose again. 'Here they come. Quick, get on the floor.'

The launch roared towards them and the captain

opened up the throttle to full. When the launch got within fifty feet a hail of bullets smashed the wheel house window-frame to pieces, showering the three men in glass.

Guy peered once again out of the cabin door, the launch suddenly pulled alongside and Otto leapt for the trawler. Shouting a warning to the Captain, Guy struggled to reach the Nazi as the Captain steered the trawler away from the launch.

Otto desperately clung to some nets which were slung ready to release, whilst the launch, which had moved out for another attack, waited as if to see what Otto would do.

The rain had made everything slippery and both men were having trouble keeping upright, let alone reaching each other. Having secured his grip, Otto reached in his pocket for his pistol. Even at fifteen feet away, he found it extremely difficult to aim at Guy who was now crouched behind a hatch. What with the heavy swell of the sea and the movement of the boat, not to mention the rain, the shot was extremely difficult. It was at this moment that Lilian chose to emerge with some caution from the cabin. From where she stood she couldn't see Otto or Guy and with great care she crossed over to the bridge.

Still holding his pistol, Otto caught sight of her and snarling with rage he took a snap shot. Guy took the opportunity to cross the deck and hurled himself at the Gestapo officer. Grasping Otto's sleeve, he desperately banged the hand holding the pistol against the iron rail. With a cry of pain the German let go of the pistol, which skated across the wet deck; savagely he grabbed Guy's hair and banged his head against the hatch cover.

At that moment the boat rolled violently as the captain steered back across the swell, causing Guy to fall backwards. He managed to drag Otto with him over the deck, but as he did so the German lashed out with his foot catching Guy across the side of his head, stunning him. They slid across the slippery surface of the deck towards the wheelhouse and Otto let go of Guy who was washed to the very edge of the deck, his feet hanging over the side of the trawler.

With a cry of triumph Otto scrambled to his feet and, clutching the safety rail, made a lunge towards the bridge after Lilian. As if on cue the launch made another dart at the trawler and the man holding the machine pistol took aim at Guy.

Suddenly, like two opposing magnets, both the trawler and the launch veered away from each other, the latter heading straight back to the shore. Lilian was still clinging to the wheelhouse door and Otto scrabbled to retrieve his pistol which was just feet away. Grasping the gun he stood up, but the look of triumph on his face turned to shock as, out of the mist and rain, the bows of a destroyer loomed into sight. What he didn't see coming was the boathook which Kitty, who had come out of the cabin, wielded with unerring accuracy. As the captain swung the trawler away from the line of the destroyer, Otto's unconscious body slid across the wet deck and narrowly missing Guy, who was still clinging on to the rail, disappeared overboard.

•

Postscript

Cannes 1958

Guy sat at the café table and thanked the waiter who set down two Manhattans. It had taken a little patience, but he sipped one and decided it had been worthwhile.

The sun beat down on the green shade above his head. It was mid summer and he now found it too much without a hat, or at least shade, for his head with his thinning hair. He watched the cameramen who were pursuing a young starlet attending the razzmatazz of the Cannes Film Festival. She was sitting on the back of a sports car, pouting her lips and pushing out two petite breasts for maximum exposure.

Guy was back in France to write an article for Life magazine, one of his last assignments before hanging up his hat for good. It had been a great career, especially the latter years when he'd worked as a freelance.

His daydreaming was suddenly startled by a kiss planted on his balding pate from behind.

'The street is a little well worn these days!'

He swung round with a grin. 'I'd recognise those lips anywhere!'

Lilian Harvey plonked herself down in the shade. 'Phew, this heat is too much for me these days. But it's lovely to see you again. How are you keeping?'

'Still surviving. Now try one of these. The barman thought I was nuts, but it's not bad.'

Lilian pulled a face. 'A Manhattan! Just a sip ... my doctor tells me they are forbidden! It's so boring, but I've already had one scare. Now - where is Kitty? And what about the children?'

'They're all fine. Currently they are in L.A. John is at Stamford and Lily is in her last year at high school. They would have come over, but it's the middle of term. Kitty sent her love and I have a pack of photos at the hotel for you.'

'So it all worked out for you and Kitty. I'm so glad.'

Guy nodded. 'After you took up war work in the States, as you know, Kitty got a small break on Broadway, which is when we got together. After the war we got married and then I went freelance. We moved to just outside Los Angeles, near Malibu, where I managed to buy a small spread. She rides everyday and we swim a lot. We're very happy.'

Lilian squeezed his arm. 'I'm delighted for you

both. I knew you would make it together and you have become quite a celebrity in your own right. I'm sure the film world is delighted you are here for the festival.`

Guy shook his head. 'That's not the reason I'm here. Life magazine has asked me to cover your life story.'

`Oh no, Guy, I'm old hat. Besides, since my time in the States I haven't done another film.'

`But you've toured on the stage. I believe you even went to Egypt at one point.'

`True, I did sing and dance for Farouk. But it wasn't the same. These days I rarely go anywhere. Next month I'm travelling to Germany to receive a lifetime award at the German Bambi film awards, which sums it all up.'

`That's great!'

Their conversation was interrupted by the starlet reappearing still sitting on the back of the car. Lilian smiled and waved, receiving a happy wave in return. `Pretty girl. I gather she will be at the Bambi awards as well, getting a newcomer's award.'

Guy watched the starlet tossing her ponytail at the photographers who buzzed around the car like bees around a honey pot. He had to admit she was pretty.

'Who is she?'

'That, my darling, is Brigitte Bardot. They say she's going to be the epitome of the swinging sixties. She comes into my boutique quite regularly, usually trailing some dishy men.'

'I wonder if they know how much we all went through,' Guy murmured, 'the murder and mayhem.'

Lilian smiled. 'I expect you'd do it all again.'

Guy laughed. 'Of course, if you were there.'

Lilian made an unladylike gesture and poked her tongue out at Guy.

Historical Note

Lilian Harvey was born Helene Lilian Muriel Pape on 19th January 1906 in Hornsey, north London, where her parents had registered their marriage.

Her mother was Ethel Marion Laughton - born 1873 in Clapton. Her maternal grandmother, Elizabeth Harvey (from whom Lilian was to take her stage surname) was born in 1847, also in Clapton, and married Daniel Laughton. They moved first to Hackney and then Islington, according to the 1891 Census.

Ethel married Walter Bruno Pape, 17th April 1897 in Islington. It is recorded that they had three children - Margaret H Pape (b.1900), Walter C Pape (b. 1903), Helene Lilian Muriel Pape (b.1906).

In 1914 the family were visiting Magdeburg,

Germany when war broke out. Unable to return to England, the two girls were sent to stay with their German aunt who lived in Solothurn, Switzerland.

After the war Helene returned to Germany and enrolled in the ballet & theatre school at Staatsoper, home of the Berlin State Opera. Unable to continue with ballet, owing to her height, she performed modern song and dance numbers with the school's touring company. Whilst they were in Vienna, Helene was spotted by a German film director, Richard Eichberg. Now using her stage name, Lilian Harvey, she was signed her up for her first movie, *Der Fluch (The Curse)*.

This tale of her life did include many well known persons and she did indeed date Gary Cooper, as well as playing opposite Sir Laurence Olivier in his first film. She was at the top of her profession in the twenties and thirties.

Her clashes with the Gestapo are well documented and Goebbels' admiration was blighted by her championing of the Jewish people, and in particular organising the escape of the choreographer, Jens Keith.

The introduction of the American journalist, Guy Parrett and Lilian's friend Kitty are figments of my imagination, as is the character Otto Heinrich, who represents the evil of the Nazi regime.

Lilian did escape to Paris, where it would have been a miracle if she had met Rick and Sam, the characters from *Casablanca,* in a jazz club! But from Paris she did go on to Antibes where she had a villa.

Here, the author takes poetic licence to get her and her friends out of France.

The reader may have noticed the surname, Harvey, which Lilian and I have in common.

In 1968 when the announcement of Lilian's death appeared in The Times, my father mentioned that not only was she a distant relative, but that he had met her many years ago, prior to her leaving for Germany. As her sister Margaret was the same age as my father, it is quite possible they had met, especially as my father attended Haberdashers' Aske's School for Boys, north of the Thames.

The last word is for 'the sweetest girl in the world'. Lilian Harvey sadly died of liver failure, at the age of sixty-two, in Juan-le-Pins, France, on the 27th July 1968.

Bernard Harvey
17th January 2017

Lightning Source UK Ltd.
Milton Keynes UK
UKOW03f0716200417
299506UK00001B/11/P